WELCOME, ANYBODY

WELCOME, ANYBODY

Stories by

JEN MCCONNELL

Press 53
Winston-Salem

Press 53, LLC
PO Box 30314
Winston-Salem, NC 27130

First Edition

Cover design by Kevin Morgan Watson

Cover art, "Young Woman Waiting" Copyright © 2012 by Gemlin,
licensed through iStockphoto

Author photo by David R. Celebrezze

Library of Congress Control Number: 2012900481

Printed on acid-free paper
ISBN 978-1-935708-49-0

for L, who lit the flame
and for DD, who keeps it burning.

Grateful acknowledgement is made to the publications where these stories first appeared:

"Debris," *Clackamas Literary Review*

"The Safest Place in the World," *Spectrum*

"Minimal," *Unknown Writer*

"The Small of Her Back," *SNReview*

"Supergirl," *The Clockhouse Review*

"What We Call Living," *Word Riot*

"Spin Cycle," *The Clockhouse Review*

"A Divorced Man's Guide to the First Year," *Flint Hills Review*

"Shakespeare's Garden," *r.kv.r.y.*

"Welcome Anybody," *Suicidally Beautiful: A Collection of Sports Stories* (Main Street Rag)

"The Last Time," *Bacopa Literary Review*

Welcome, Anybody

DEBRIS

S heryl stood over the cowboy on the steps of the dirty stage and kicked him with the toe of her platform shoe. He didn't move. She looked around the room at the crowd heading for the exits, leaving the two of them alone with the vacant tables and littered floor. Sheryl could still see their blank faces and fingers that itched for what came next. She'd served cocktails at the Paradise Lounge for two years and it was always the same: no matter what happened during the night, everyone looked alike when the house lights came on. Except for the cowboy.

Sheryl preferred working in the main room with its two-story ceiling, purplish lighting and clouds of stale smoke because she could move unaccosted, unlike in the Catwalk. The front entrance of the Paradise Lounge led to the Catwalk, a long narrow bar where men lined up to grope women as they squeezed by. Sheryl didn't walk through there during her shift and avoided the back room as well, the Transmission Theater, which was devoted to speed metal and recreational drugs. The stage in the main room, offering a rotation of local bands, provided almost enough entertainment to distract Sheryl from her own life.

She pushed the cowboy over, her bracelets jangling in the deserted room. His skinny body gave way easily under her fingers. She heard Dudley's whistling and the clank of glassware behind the bar. Sheryl ran her finger down the cowboy's pale, freckled cheekbone but he didn't open his eyes. The hat was gone and his red hair was moist and flat against his head. His neck arched awkwardly, as if his head was about to snap off and roll across the floor.

Sheryl pressed two fingers into the cowboy's wrist and felt a faint throbbing. She closed her eyes and ignored her own heartbeat, the way she learned in nursing school. There was no second pulse. His skin was cold now, clammy, no longer hot and electric. Dudley called to her.

"He's dead," she answered.

Dudley's laugh echoed across the empty room. "They're all like that," he said. But when he came and stood over them, his sharp eyes narrowed. He lifted the cowboy's arm. It dropped heavily to the floor. "Holy shit."

Dudley dialed the phone as Sheryl retreated behind the bar and sipped gin from a cracked coffee mug.

The cowboy was much nicer when he was still, Sheryl decided. He was smaller and less threatening. She thought for a moment that she had somehow caused this.

The crowd had been the usual Saturday night poseurs. Hi-tech boys from the Peninsula, dressed in shorts and plaid shirts, watched the band from the back of the room. Hipsters ordered highballs for their dates in fishnets and Mary Janes. A guy with a nose ring and ripped jeans drank tequila shots and asked Sheryl for her phone number. She ignored him.

Sheryl noticed the cowboy and his friends when they staggered in during the opening band's set, shouting their order at her. The cowboy wore a leather jacket with silver buckles and a dirty white cowboy hat, the kind they used to sell at the flea market on Van Ness. They drank three rounds of Bud in less than an hour. Sheryl lost track of them until the headliner began to play. During the first song, the cowboy made his way through the crowd and climbed up the steps to the stage, mindless of the hipsters swinging their girls around the dance floor. He stood on the top step and shook his fist in front of the lead singer's face, yelling "You got it!" and "You crazy mother-fucker."

Sheryl watched the dancers move away from the cowboy as he staggered down the steps, clobbering people with his upraised arms. As Sheryl squeezed between people to clear glasses from the front of the stage, she overheard a girl yell into her boyfriend's ear, "No fighting!" Sheryl saw the gleam in the boy's eyes as the cowboy bumped into him. The club had its own set of rules and the crowd didn't like them broken by an outsider. There was a quickness in the cowboy—Sheryl sensed it, too—a grasping for something that they could not reach. Sheryl almost wished that a fight would break out so he would be taken away. It happened before.

Later, while the band played an encore, Sheryl escaped down the back hallway and through the propped open emergency exit to smoke in the empty night. Against the rough wall, she could feel the thump of the bass drum in her heart. People walked by on the sidewalk, talking and laughing, as the January cold crawled up her bare legs. Sheryl imagined them going to parties or Denny's or to bed. People were the same everywhere. San Francisco was no different than Pittsburgh or Miami, none of which she had ever considered home.

When the band finished and Dudley shouted last call, the crowd thinned out. Sheryl was clearing a table when the cowboy lurched into her. He wasn't wearing the jacket and the sleeves of his 1987 AC/DC T-shirt were rolled up to the elbows. His black jeans were filthy and frayed and the cowboy hat was pulled low over his eyes.

"Where's the toilet?" he asked.

He was touching her. A slight pressure of his hand encircling her naked wrist. Sheryl stood still and tried to remember the last person who had touched her. The cowboy's eyes were barely visible under the brim of the hat but she could see his full pink lips. He smiled down at her like a child coveting a favorite marble.

"Shiny…skinny." He stroked the inside of her wrist with his fingers. "Mine."

Sheryl turned her wrist sharply and grabbed his hand. The cowboy growled in the back of his throat and let her lead him down the hallway. She pushed him into the door of the men's room.

"Thanks, darlin'," he drawled, stumbling backward through the door.

Sheryl pulled one of the bracelets from her left wrist to her right, covering the part of her he touched. By the time Dudley yelled at her twenty minutes later to wake up the drunk on the stage, Sheryl had almost forgotten about the cowboy.

After the ambulance left, Sheryl said goodbye to Dudley.

"Are you sure you're okay?" he called over his shoulder. "If you stay awhile, I'll give you a ride."

The words hung between them as she watched his shoulders hitch up awkwardly. He was more disturbed than she was, Sheryl thought as she left the main room. She doubted he'd ever seen a dead body before. As much as he tried to blend into San Francisco, Sheryl knew deep down he was just a nice boy from Ohio.

Max, the janitor, swept litter and broken glass into a heap as Sheryl passed through the Catwalk. He motioned to her. The cowboy's jacket lay on top of the bar.

Though he kept all the money he found, Max always gave Sheryl the pick of the night's leftovers. The rough burlap bag she carried was a find from October. In the last two years, Sheryl took home three purses, a charm bracelet, an empty locket and a short baby-blue leather skirt. Max had found the skirt outside on the sidewalk. At first it repulsed Sheryl to wear castaway clothing but it fit her perfectly. She picked up the jacket and nodded to Max, who resumed sweeping. He was her only friend.

Under the amber streetlights, Sheryl smoked, watching the traffic lights flash yellow and the neon lights of the dance clubs turn off. She shivered and slipped into the jacket. The leather was cold on her arms and neck and she could smell the cowboy's scent: smoky and dark, like the back corner of the club. When she heard Dudley say goodbye to Max, she turned toward downtown.

She would take the cowboy's jacket to the hospital and leave it with the rest of his things. Looking up at the sky, she counted twelve stars in the fading night. The clock in the Bank of the Orient building read four o'clock. Sheryl was past the point of sleeping, the time when the buildings and the cars and the street people began to look like family.

In front of St. Francis Hospital, Sheryl lit another cigarette, shielding the match against the wind that stirred the debris around her. The jacket warmed her, the buckles jangling softly as she shifted from foot to foot. She blew on her dry, cold hands, almost missing the punishing heat of the desert.

She left Reno two years earlier to get as far west as she could without drowning. She had settled into the worn seat of a Greyhound bus. The hours, like the landscape, passed slowly. Eventually the barren desert gave way to naked summer mountains, highway towns, beige suburbs and finally, the San Francisco Bay.

During the bus ride, she pulled out her address book and considered each name written on its flowered pages. The names brought up images—smoking pot at the bowling alley, eating bin food at the Piggly Wiggly—but the faces remained blurred. Was that Jimmy in Des Moines or Ray in Miami? When each entry was scratched off, Sheryl ripped the page in half.

She wrote down the two names she wanted to keep— Gramma in Florida and her sister Lonnie in Iowa—in a small, unlined notebook. Lonnie probably spent Christmases with Gramma. Sheryl imagined them driving together to the grocery store where Lonnie would make sure Gramma used her coupons. Lonnie had always been the patient one.

By the time Sheryl reached San Francisco, where the buildings were tall enough to hide her, the floor underneath her seat was littered with paper. After stepping out of the Transbay Terminal, she spent the early Sunday morning walking through downtown. She peeked through the windows of deserted banks and restaurants and office buildings. This time, she promised herself, she would not touch anything.

In the basement of the hospital, Sheryl stopped at a desk in the corridor and signed her name to the list of visitors, hesitating at the 'relationship to deceased' box. Behind the desk, a fat black-haired woman was reading a magazine. She looked up at Sheryl and smiled sadly, her chin jiggling as she spoke.

"You're here for the young man they brought in, aren't you? Girlfriend?"

The guard checked her watch. There was probably someone waiting for her at home, Sheryl thought. Someone who would make fresh coffee and talk to her in the kitchen as the sun came up. The guard would tell a story about a dead cowboy and his girlfriend.

"Yes," Sheryl whispered.

The woman handed Sheryl a pink tissue from a box on the desk.

"I'm sorry, honey," she said. "Is there someone else to call?"

"Please." Sheryl remembered the cowboy's smile when he touched her. "I'm all he has."

The guard sighed, hauled herself out of the chair and pushed open the swinging doors. Sheryl stopped inside the room as the guard motioned to a table draped with a white sheet.

"Let me know if you need me," the guard whispered.

The sparseness of the narrow room stretched away from Sheryl. It was the cleanest room she'd ever been in. No wastebasket, no lint on the tiled floor, no color or dirt anywhere. Just four stainless steel tables gleaming under the lights, empty except for the one in front of her. There was no smell either except the scent of the club that Sheryl brought with her.

As she moved toward the covered table, Sheryl wiped her hands on her skirt. She wondered if they threw away the sheets that touched the bodies or just bleached them or if they even distinguished between these sheets and those for live patients. Maybe they all just blurred together.

She took off the leather jacket and laid it near the cowboy's feet. Gingerly, she lifted the sheet and looked at his bare chest. He was even skinnier than she imagined; she could probably span his waist with her hands. She could see the ridges of his ribs and a reddish-brown mole on his neck. She tried to remember the faces of his friends, wondering how they could leave him to die in a dirty anonymous club.

It had been two hours since she found the cowboy. He looked the same, only paler. The freckles on his face stood out in relief against his cheekbones and his eyelashes were so fair she could hardly see them. Pulling the sheet off completely, Sheryl looked at his naked body and wondered if he was a good lover. If he'd hold her close, breathing gently into her face so she could taste him and stroking her cheek as he came inside her. They would fall asleep together tangled in the sheets of her twin bed. He'd make up stories to entertain her and call her "darlin'" in his low voice.

She rested her head on the cowboy's chest and stroked his cold arms. The tears trickled down her cheeks, pooling on his chest. For a moment she imagined she felt the mingling of their heartbeats.

She jerked up at the scrape of the guard's chair on the floor and the jingling of her keys. Sheryl let go of the cowboy and picked up the jacket. She pulled it on slowly, rubbing the leather with her hands to warm it before she walked outside.

The Safest Place in the World

As we waited in the hallway of the emergency room, I struggled to rub lavender lotion on my legs, unable to bear my dry skin a moment longer. Ryan slumped in a nearby chair, his hand hidden under a bag of ice chips. His face was pale, his blue T-shirt had dark circles under the arms and his sweaty hair needed a trim.

It was Sunday; Ryan had been emptying out the walk-in coat closet. We were turning it into a nursery. I was downstairs doing laundry when I heard him shouting. I was afraid something like this would happen.

Behind us a man on a gurney with an IV laced to his hand began to moan. Two orderlies, one in green scrubs and the other in orange, walked by carrying stacks of clean linens. I shrunk back against the wall, trying to pull my pregnant stomach out of the way.

"Feng shui," Green said. He took a towel from the stack and wiped his bald head. "Only ballpark in America with genuine feng shui compatibility."

"What do you know about feng shui?" Orange snorted at him. "Just need Barry Bonds' bat and the short porch in right."

They stopped at a closet next to Ryan, their clogs squeaking on the tile. "Season starts in a couple weeks," Green said. "You'll see."

I bent down to Ryan. "Do you believe in feng shui, honey?"

"This city's too small to believe in stuff like that." He didn't open his eyes.

"It doesn't matter the size," I said.

"You have too much time on your hands," Ryan whispered.

"Some people take it seriously. The Japanese. Or maybe it's the Chinese..."

The orderlies, ignoring us and the man groaning on the gurney, continued down the hallway.

"Hell," Green said. "I heard of a guy, changed his whole business around, an auto body shop. Next day, boom, won the lottery."

Ryan's voice drowned out Orange's reply. "You read too much into things, sweetie," he said. "It's just a broken finger."

"You know it's more than that."

"An accident."

I wanted to say more but the man on the gurney began to yell something in a slurred voice. A nurse, who reminded me of a redheaded penguin, glided out of the nearest room on a stool with wheels and snapped the gloves off his hands. He gently pushed the man back down on the gurney.

"Something's wrong," the man said. "My leg."

The nurse hushed him and rolled over to us. He read Ryan's chart.

"A box of books?" He lifted the ice bag.

Ryan shrugged and held up his hand. The middle finger was bent like a lightning bolt.

"He just didn't want to paint the baby's room," I said.

"I told you," Ryan said. "I didn't realize the box was up there."

Behind us, the man banged the IV cart against the gurney.

"Hey, buddy," the nurse called out, never taking his eyes from Ryan's hand. "Stay in bed."

"I have to go," the man wheezed.

Ryan looked up at me and we pretended not to listen.

"I know." The nurse released Ryan's hand and rolled over

to the gurney. "But you have three choices. You can go back on the street where it's cold. You can go to jail. Or you can stay in a nice warm bed. Hospital's the safest place in the world, right?"

I turned to watch the man's response. I expected him to be sprawled in the gurney but he was sitting up straight and looking at me with surprising clarity in his blue eyes. His gaze went right through me—into my worries about the laundry wrinkling in the dryer and the chicken I forgot to defrost—and paused long enough to make me glance away. When I looked back, the man's attention had moved on to the troublesome IV tangled around his arm. He began picking at the tape that held the needle in place. I stared at his trembling hands, imagining his arm hair slowly being ripped from the skin. After a few minutes, he gave up and lay back down.

"Safest place in the world," he mumbled.

The nurse re-wrapped the ice around Ryan's hand.

"We'll take an x-ray," he said. "Looks like a clean break. Get it wrapped up. Then we'll get you home safe and sound, okay?"

Night had fallen by the time we arrived home. Ryan pushed coats and umbrellas off the sofa with his uninjured hand and lay down. I moved to pick them up but he waved me away.

"Take a bath." He closed his eyes. "It's your turn, you know."

"Don't say that," I said. "We have to do something."

"Bad luck, sweetie."

"Four trips to the ER in one year?" I asked. "That's some bad luck."

"Do you really believe it's all connected?"

I looked around the room. Furniture and baby things covered every inch of the floor. Every surface was crowded with picture frames and plants and books. I constantly reorganized closets and cabinets to make more room. Now six months pregnant, I felt squeezed out of the life the two of us had begun together, but I was afraid to tell Ryan what I believed.

In the bathtub, I rubbed soap across my belly. When I was first pregnant, I couldn't wait until my baby belly showed. It didn't seem real until there was a physical change. Now, the bigger I got, the more worried I became. I couldn't imagine how we would all fit together.

I thought of the orderlies at the hospital. Maybe it was that easy. Maybe all I had to do was move the sofa and a lamp and life would fit together again. I had tried everything else: horseshoes, incense, a rabbit foot. Couldn't hurt, I thought.

The next evening after work, I moved quickly through the apartment before Ryan came home. I knew almost nothing about feng shui but enough to know we weren't doing it.

I stood next to the sofa and peered at Ryan's Van Gogh painting called *Wheat Field with Crows*, a cheap museum print in a ten-dollar frame he had since high school. The wheat field was dark brown and gold with two dozen black crows darkening the blue sky. Ryan said it made him feel calm but I always imagined that the crows were coming after me.

In the garage downstairs, I looked at the space we shared with our upstairs neighbors. In the space next to our neighbors' car, the washer and dryer were jammed between mountain bikes, boxes of wedding china and Ryan's baseball card collection. He hadn't looked at a single card in twenty years and we'd never broken the seal on the china.

What had once seemed necessary—a rice cooker, power sander, ice cream maker, exercise bike—I forgot we even had. I eyed our neighbors' neatly stacked boxes, wondering how they managed life with such few possessions.

The rest of the week, I spent the evenings sorting through our boxes in the garage and the closets upstairs, trying to remember why we had so many things.

The next Saturday afternoon, I carried two bags of clothes to Goodwill, then stopped at the bookstore to pick out a book on feng shui. The clerk at the register, fingering the belly ring on her firm, flat stomach, glanced at my selection.

"Wait 'til you're done," she said. "You won't believe the rush."

"You've done it, too?" I whispered.

"My whole apartment. It's a shrine now. Calm, serene. I could invite the Dalai Lama over." She lowered her voice. "I want to do this place but they won't let me." She tapped on the counter, a thick wood rectangle in the center of the store. "Can't you feel the difference in the chi when you step in here? It's not right. Like you're suddenly walking underwater."

I nodded and hurried home. While Ryan was off grocery shopping, I moved from room to room with the book in one hand and a notepad in the other. According to the Bagua map, nearly everything in our apartment was wrong. Not the stuff that had always bothered me—the hum of the refrigerator, the mismatched tiles in the kitchen or the bathroom window leading only to an airshaft. Even a closet turned into a nursery didn't matter as long as it followed the rules. It was the shape and placement of the furniture. The colors and fabrics. They all contributed or interfered with the chi—the life force, the energy—of our home and lives.

As I suspected, the Van Gogh was completely inappropriate. Though a picture of the landscape was encouraged, it should be soft, tranquil colors with round or oval shapes. Swimming fish were preferable. Not frightening crows over a deserted wheat field in a cheap replica of a painting by a long-dead artist. It would have to go.

Inside the hall closet, books were still sprawled on the floor. I packed them back into the boxes and closed the door. They would have to wait until Ryan's hand healed. In the living room, I pushed the coffee table to the wall under the bay window, how it was when we first moved in. Now it barely fit, crowded between everything else but already the room felt roomier, calmer. I closed my eyes and imagined the chi running through me.

At six o'clock, I was lying on the couch reading when I heard Ryan's key in the lock. I hurried to hide the book in the laundry basket. When I came out of the bathroom, Ryan was in the living room, looking at the coffee table under the window. I wanted to tell him what I'd done but looking at his puzzled face, I knew he wouldn't understand.

"Spring cleaning," I said.

"It's barely March."

"Nesting, then."

He reached over the sofa and straightened the Van Gogh with his good hand.

"It was just a broken finger," he said.

The days took on a new rhythm as I spent hours secretly purging the apartment. I rearranged the furniture a dozen times trying to follow the rules. Every Saturday I took a bag of clothing and books to Goodwill and each Sunday fell asleep planning the next week's chores.

Some nights I turned the Giants' game on while I cleaned. Ryan questioned my newfound interest in baseball but didn't complain. They lost their first sixteen games and there was never any mention of feng shui at the new stadium. I wondered if the orderlies had made it up.

After six weeks, the apartment was more spacious and all that remained was to take down the Van Gogh. When Ryan asked about something that was missing, I told him I was baby-proofing. He didn't ask about the furniture being moved. I began to believe we had made our last trip to the ER.

Four weeks from my due date, Ryan asked if we could go for a walk. I was delighted with his unexpected attention. We poked through the neighborhood stores, avoiding the hills I could no longer climb, and then drank iced coffee outside Martha Brothers.

"Penelope?" Ryan plucked at a daisy he'd bought for me.

"Penny? No." I held a petal to my nose. It smelled of grass and pollen. "How about Meredith."

"Allison."

"I thought we liked Meredith?"

"Something more peaceful." He pointed to the coffee store sign. "How about Martha? She makes good coffee."

"What about Grace? Or does it sound like we're trying to dictate her personality?"

"Grace. That's nice."

"Boy names now," I said.

He dropped the flower stem to the ground, his face more serious than normal. "Can I tell you something?" he asked.

I nodded, nervous that he was going to ask about the apartment.

"Do you remember that little blond girl at your cousin's wedding?" he continued. "How she stood on her father's feet while they danced? Her feet were so small on his shoes."

"Isabel," I said. "That's a good name."

"I can't stop thinking about her. You know why? Because that's what I want." He took a sip of coffee. "You know when you fainted last Thanksgiving? I felt like such a failure. I was standing right next to you and I couldn't save you. I think, for a little while at least, I could protect a little girl."

"Why are you telling me this?" I asked. "What if we have a boy?"

"It's different with boys."

"You mean you wouldn't protect a boy?" I pulled my hand away but he held tight.

"It's not that," Ryan said. "I just wanted to tell you. It's something you should know. That's what I want, I can't help it. What do you want, really?"

I closed my eyes and brought a petal to my nose. The scent was gone but I could still taste it in the back of my throat. Ryan pulled me to him. I buried my face in his chest, smelling the heavy sweat on his skin. We had agreed we didn't care what the baby was as long as it was healthy. Having a preference, I thought, would be dangerous.

"It's okay, sweetie," he said. "I won't think anything bad."

"A girl," I whispered, rubbing his hand. There was a small indentation on the knuckle where the bone had been broken. The doctor said it would always be that way. "I'd love a little girl, too."

He hugged me. "We can tell each other these things. It doesn't change anything."

We held hands as we walked home and it finally felt as if we were in this together. Ryan grinned as he opened the front door and my mother and sister loomed toward us, vivacious in their flowered dresses and bright lipstick. Behind them, the living room overflowed with women.

"Surprise," Candace, my sister, shouted as Ryan backed out the door.

I wanted to go with him rather than be in my own home, for my own surprise baby shower, with my family and friends and all their gifts. The apartment had been perfect when we left—cool and airy and welcoming, the chi flowing freely.

Now the windows were closed and steamy with humidity. The coffee table was pulled into the middle of the room and piled with baby gifts. Pink and blue streamers were draped from the Van Gogh to the mirror over the television and back. A rocking chair sat where the coffee table had been, a red ribbon draped across it.

"Surprised, sugar?" My mother hugged me.

"What'd you do to the place?" Candace asked. "I couldn't find the cake platter."

"It must be...I think it's wrapped up. I'll look for it." I had given it away. We never used it and it took up half a pantry shelf. As I turned toward the kitchen, my mother grabbed my hand. "I'm thirsty, Mom," I said.

"You just relax, honey," she said. "Have some of Ruth's famous punch and you'll be fine. Sans champagne, of course." She laughed, a thick cackle in the hot room. "You have presents to open."

"I can't." I rushed to the bathroom, locked the door and vomited into the toilet.

My family loved to throw parties. It didn't matter if I was there or not. They didn't know that what I wanted most was the three of us—Ryan, me and the baby—safe and sound in our own home. I ignored the pounding on the bathroom door and opened the window. The cool wind dried the sweat on my face. Eventually I heard my mother usher the guests out. Finally, Ryan called to me.

"They're all gone, sweetheart. It's just us."

I opened the door. The baby gifts were stacked by the rocking chair: enough clothes, toys and books for a dozen children. I held my breath while Ryan shoved them into the nursery closet and closed the door.

Two weeks later, voices from upstairs woke me long after midnight. The evening had been warm enough to leave the windows open and sounds drifted in piece by piece. I listened to the laughter, thinking about how well the nursery closet had turned out. The sage green paint was a soothing complement to the gray carpet. A triangular window high in the corner provided soft light once Ryan removed the shelves. I returned most of the gifts from the baby shower. The chi flowed freely through all the rooms.

The Van Gogh was the last thing to go. Of course Ryan would notice but I found a replacement at a consignment shop, an oil painting of pink and yellow fish. He would like it once it was on the wall, I told myself.

I slipped out of bed and went into the living room. Now the crows in the Van Gogh seemed to be flying away from me toward the full yellow moon on the horizon. That was a good sign but I couldn't wait any longer. I grabbed the edge of the frame, arching up to lift it off the hooks. That's when the contraction came, making me drop the Van Gogh. The frame hit my foot before crashing to the floor. The glass shattered into pieces. Ryan appeared next to me, reaching for my hand as I bent over, clutching at my stomach and moaning.

"Are you okay?" he said.

"It has to go," I whispered.

"Are you okay?" he repeated.

"Contraction."

"I'll get the car." He pulled on shoes as he ran out the door.

I sat on the couch looking at the glass and the Van Gogh print, which had popped out of the frame. At least it was off the wall now, I thought. When the next contraction subsided, I examined my foot. The skin wasn't broken but it had begun to swell.

At the hospital, the registration nurse greeted us by name but I didn't recognize the orderly who wheeled me to maternity. Ryan wouldn't sit down or even lean against the wall.

"You don't know what you might catch," he whispered.

I wondered where the man with the IV had gone. As safe as the hospital was, no one could stay forever. I studied the room while the doctor examined me. The metal trays had rough, sharp edges and the exam table jutted into the middle of the room. Was it possible to have a feng shui hospital? Would the decreased efficiency be offset by increased chi? Suddenly, I was exhausted and my foot was throbbing.

The doctor told us the baby could come at any time.

"You're about four centimeters," he said. "Come back if the contractions start again."

"She doesn't have to stay here?" Ryan asked, taking my hand.

"Could be tonight. Could be another week." The doctor turned to me. "Unless you want to stay."

I looked down at Ryan's hand. Only he and I would ever be able to tell which finger had been broken. I shook my head.

The doctor prescribed a nightly bath and half a glass of wine. It didn't occur to me until we were in the car to ask if it should be red or white wine but I didn't want to go back. Ryan hunched over the steering wheel, his greasy hair hanging into his eyes. He used to get his hair cut every four weeks but was off-schedule ever since he broke his finger.

Ryan ran the bath while I poured two glasses of red wine. As he helped me into the tub, I noticed the dark circles under his eyes. I offered to cut his hair.

"Tomorrow." He took a sip of wine, then raised himself up and snapped off the light. He rested his hand on my stomach. "How do you feel?" he asked.

"I don't want to go the hospital anymore," I said.

"Just once more. But for a good reason, right?"

"Will you throw out the Van Gogh?"

"They were just accidents."

"I know it means something to you, but it's...I can't explain it."

"You should have just told me."

"That was the last thing."

"I know," he said. "The place looks great."

"Can you feel it?"

"You can tell me everything," he said.

I nodded and sipped the wine. Moonlight eased in between the parted curtain as the bath water grew cold. Ryan helped me out of the tub. I rested my hand on his shoulder for balance and began to dry my legs. When I looked up, Ryan was watching me, tears glittering in his eyes.

He took the towel from me and rubbed my stomach.

Later, in bed, I knew he would listen while I told him everything and we would gently fall asleep but for now there was only the sweet pressure of his hands circling across me.

Minimal

E verything was under control until Conrad dropped the hairbrush. One of Sarah's earrings, a single diamond with no backing, lay under the sink in the grout between the dull white tiles. Conrad thought he'd gotten rid of everything. He sat on the toilet lid staring at the earring in his hand until he noticed the *SF Weekly* in the trashcan. In the midst of all the sex ads in the back, he was caught by the name Bernadette. He could lose himself in a woman like that, he thought. Different than hard, petite Sarah.

A few hours later, the doorbell rang.

"Like ordering a pizza," Conrad whispered.

Bernadette's tall figure and voluminous red hair filled the doorway, like some genie he conjured up. He stared at her leopard print purse as her eyes skipped past him into the bare apartment.

"We're going out then?" she asked, her voice softer than he would have guessed.

Conrad staggered forward a bit. She backed up into the hallway.

"Her fucking diamond earring," he said, holding out his left hand. "Christmas present from her parents. I could have found it before today but I didn't. It's a sign. She's back from Hawaii today—her honeymoon. I thought after she was married things would be different. There'd be some sort of closure. But instead, it feels like it's just beginning." He closed his eyes and leaned against the doorjamb.

"I'm here to help you forget her?" she asked.

He shook his head. It sounded so simple in his mind.

After Sarah left his apartment for the last time, Conrad had binged on cleaning. He mopped and bleached and repainted every inch of his studio apartment stinging white. He left the windows open at night to chill the metal surfaces of the eat-in kitchen. It took a week to give everything away, just long enough to lose his job and miss two auditions. Now there was only the naked bed wedged into the walk-in closet and a second-hand stereo on the floor under the bay window. He would leave those behind when he left.

"They got engaged about a year ago." He sat down in the doorway. Bernadette squatted next to him, pulling her skirt over her knees and gesturing for him to continue. "I liked her. We fooled around. Snuck around, hung out, fucked. Whatever you want to call it. The whole time she was going out with Ben. Maybe she was in love with me but I didn't feel anything. Not enough, anyway. Not like I should have." He looked at the earring in his hand, like a hungry dog caught in a rainstorm. "She wanted me to stop her from marrying him. I know that now. Maybe that was my chance and I blew it. I want to tell her that." Conrad looked into Bernadette's wide green eyes. She wasn't shocked or even interested. She'd heard better, he thought, and worse.

He stood up and threw the earring into the apartment. It made a tiny sound on the bare wood floor.

"Let's go," he said.

They rode the bus through Chinatown to North Beach. The T-shirt and trinket shops had grown quiet. Always in that corner of the city it sounded as if something was happening ten minutes away. At the intersection of Columbus and Broadway, Conrad felt the urge to run after the voices that turned into deserted alleyways. Sarah could be one of them. On the streets around them, *maitre d's* urged them into restaurants, bums held out their hands and strippers stood behind burly-armed men who shouted *Ladies get in free!* She could be here. When the light turned green, Bernadette tugged on his jacket and led him to the restaurant.

"I've never been to this one," she said. "I hear it's good." Her voice was low and even, like a white noise machine blocking everything out for an instant—this was a normal conversation, they were having a normal date, he could enjoy this—then it all came roaring back.

"Anything you want," he answered. "Feel free."

Inside, wait staff glided silently between the crowded tables. Conrad shifted back and forth on his toes, cracking his knuckles.

"Maybe this wasn't a good idea," he whispered. He turned to leave but Bernadette was already following the hostess. Maybe he didn't need her for this but he knew, because that's how life worked, that if he did see Sarah and he was alone, then nothing would ever change. He would have to hold it all inside from then on.

Bernadette looked back at him. In another minute she would become embarrassed. A waiter stepped up and spoke Conrad's name though his lips didn't seem to move. He was a friend of Sarah's. Conrad followed him to the table.

"You just missed her," the waiter said. "She had pictures of the wedding. She looked beautiful."

Conrad spoke too loudly. "What're the specials, all right? We're in a hurry."

Bernadette watched closely as Conrad ordered for both of them. He guessed correctly that she was a vegetarian. A sensitive sex worker, he thought. Of course.

"So," he said.

"You have great eyes, you know. I was looking at them. Very deep."

"They're just brown."

"No, really. The lashes—I wish mine were so thick."

"Stop it." He gulped his icy cocktail. He forgot what he ordered and couldn't taste anything discernible. "It's not necessary." His mother had teased him as a child about his girl eyes. They were the only feature that distinguished him from everybody else. His average hair, average height and average face were ideal for the bit parts he picked up in commercials.

"Tell me about her." Bernadette reached out her hand.

Conrad ignored it and sipped his drink. "She lived…lives…just a few blocks away. I figured she'd come here on their first night back. She loves this place. Ben didn't like fancy restaurants so we went without him. She paid and he had no idea that I would take her home later and fuck her." He looked up at Bernadette, the light from the candle on the table reflected in her eyes.

"About six weeks ago, I walked by this place and saw them in here together." He ran his fingers across the candle's flame. "They were at a table in the front window. I saw Ben brush the hair out of her eyes. He'd probably done it a million times. The look on her face…I should have been jealous. I mean, we had something, whatever it was." He drained his glass and wiped his mouth with the back of his hand. "She saw me. Smiled at me over his shoulder. I knew she wanted me to come in, burst in like a jealous lover or something. I pretended I didn't see her because I didn't want that then. But I knew, if she called me later, I'd go over and spend the night with her."

"Did you?"

He nodded. "We never mentioned the restaurant. That night, after she fell asleep, I stayed awake, trying to remember the last time I wanted a woman in a way I couldn't explain rationally."

He hadn't touched Sarah until she touched him first, months after Ben had been established as the boyfriend. Conrad didn't understand why she would cheat but he was ravenous after all her flirting. She wanted him, so why should it be on his conscience? If he suspected she would really marry Ben, maybe he would have been more insistent on coming clean. But he hadn't wanted her that badly. Now, though it had only been a few weeks, parts of her—her skin, hair, lips—were already fading from his memory. Maybe touches, sounds and smells had to be repeated continuously or they were forgotten. Once, about a year after his mother had left, Conrad's father told him that she was dead. It was easier for both of them.

"Taste this." Bernadette offered her fork across the table, smearing a drop of oil on Conrad's lip. He bit into the pasta. "Isn't that good?"

He'd eaten that dish before, ravioli in a lemon cream sauce. It had never tasted so good. "Yes," he said and ate another forkful from her plate. When he finished, he motioned for the check. There were so many places to go.

Outside, Bernadette shivered and Conrad handed her his jacket. She slipped it over her full shoulders and shook her hair from the collar.

"You're beautiful," he said, trying to believe the sincerity of his own voice.

They took BART to Casanova's in the Mission. Red lights bathed the bar and everyone seemed to glow. A stage in the back was draped with heavy black curtains. There was nowhere to go in the crush of people.

"She's here," Conrad shouted over the music. He felt like a dog on a trail. "Or at least she was."

"How do you know?"

"My stomach hurts. My stomach never hurts, but now…"

"Maybe it was the food."

"What?"

Near the back of the bar, Bernadette pushed Conrad onto a red velvet couch and squeezed onto his lap.

"When were you here last?" she asked.

"Three days before her wedding," he said. "I told her it was her private bachelorette party. We drank cosmos so sweet they made my teeth ache. She was giddy. I took her to bed later."

"Tell me what you told her."

"What?"

A waitress leaned over the back of the couch. Conrad shook his head as Bernadette ordered two cosmos.

"Tell me the same things you told her. Pretend it's that night." She raised her voice an octave. "I can't believe I'm going to be married and you aren't going to do anything about it." She kissed his ear.

"Don't be stupid." Conrad pulled away.

"Pretend I'm her."

"That's not how it works," he said.

"Then why'd you call me?"

"I needed company and I don't mind paying for it."

"What do you feel, really, right now?"

He looked away from Bernadette, into the laughing, jostling crowd. That last night with Sarah, he felt relief. Her wedding was something definitive. In the morning, as she stirred next to him, he lost himself for a moment as he looked at her face in the sunlight.

"Maybe I should have asked you," he had whispered. "Ben's not the one for you. My timing was wrong, is all."

She opened her eyes and threw off the covers. "Don't tell me that now, jerk. It's too late."

"Is it?"

She picked up a pillow from the floor and threw it at him. "Shut up. That's convenient for you, isn't it? I don't want to hear it."

He watched her pull on her clothes, her mouth set tight, uninviting, and so he laughed as if it had all been a joke. That was the last time he saw her. Conrad was telling this to Bernadette when something caught his attention over her shoulder.

"It's her." He started to move but Bernadette kissed him, her mouth hot and sweet.

Conrad pulled back and looked at Sarah but it wasn't her. The woman turned back to her friends at the bar.

"Don't lose it." Bernadette pressed her hand into his thigh. His face flared up as he pulled her off the couch.

Bernadette suggested they go to Café Macondo but Conrad wasn't listening. He led her down Valencia, stopping in front of the consignment shop at Seventeenth Street. He pointed to a ruby necklace in the window. The deep red jewel was shaped like a teardrop and threaded onto a simple gold chain. It looked so real it had to be fake.

"Sarah loved jewelry," he said. "Ben never gave her any. She complained all the time about how cheap he was."

An old man was pulling the metal gate across the door. Conrad motioned to him and they went inside. It took only a minute to buy the necklace.

"She'd point this one out every time we passed by. I was going to surprise her someday but she never gave me the chance." He pulled Bernadette under the streetlight and clasped the chain around her neck. He lifted the ruby with his fingers. "It's perfect on you."

"I can't keep this."

"It's for you."

"I know you wish I were her," Bernadette whispered. "That's okay."

When they stepped into Timo's down the street, the aqua green and blue tiles on the floor reminded Conrad of a deep swimming pool. Bernadette ordered shots of tequila. Conrad's eyes shone behind his long lashes.

"That last night together," he said, "after we made love, she told me we could still be friends."

"All women say that," Bernadette said.

"But she didn't mean it."

"No one does." Bernadette shifted from foot to foot, like grains of sand pouring back and forth.

"She's everywhere," he said. "But I can't get it all together."

"Why does it have to be tonight?"

"I'm leaving tomorrow."

"For where?"

"Somewhere new."

"Running away just because of a girl?"

"You don't understand."

"Don't I?"

They looked at each other for a moment. Conrad expected her to look away but she held his gaze. He noticed a faint birthmark on her cheek, a spot of skin slightly paler than the rest of her face.

"I read once," Bernadette said, "that the minimal pulse for humans to survive is forty beats a minute. Anything above that is gratuitous."

Conrad pushed his empty glass away.

"Do you understand what I'm saying?" she asked. "Just let it be for a while. You'll bounce back."

He traced his finger along Bernadette's cheek. She didn't flinch and continued to look him square in the eyes. An image of the endless desert floated in his mind, the hills that looked close enough to touch but really were hours away.

"It's not about bouncing back," he said. "Let's go home."

"Already?" She grasped his hand and held it against her face. "She could be right around the corner."

For two years, he and Sarah had crisscrossed the city, going to movies and restaurants and bars to fill up the space between them. Conrad thought he'd been satisfied with having only those pieces of her.

"I still have the bed," Conrad said to Bernadette, pulling her off the barstool. "It's in the closet."

They waited around the corner for the 22 Fillmore. Bernadette pointed to a brick building across the street that rose above a brightly lit Laundromat. She lived on the third floor.

"But you're coming home with me," he said, closing his hand on her arm. He wanted her now, suddenly. The hair on his arms and neck stood up. Bernadette moved close to him and put her hand on his shoulder. He kissed her, tasting her breath and lipstick, feeling the heat of her cheek and the density of her hair. He definitely could lose himself in her.

As they boarded the bus, he turned to help her up. Looking past her, he saw Sarah walking into the bar behind the bus shelter. The windows were completely black but white light poured out of the open door. She was grasping the arm of someone in front of her. He was sure it was Sarah; he saw her whole face—the black curtain of hair, the bubblegum curve of her cheek. She looked straight at him, her eyes floating up and down his body but nothing registered in her eyes or manner. She stepped through the door and disappeared. Conrad made no movement as the bus rocked up to speed.

He would ride with Bernadette to the naked apartment

and take her into the closet. He would remove her clothes in the cool, textured darkness where there would be no distractions. It would be quiet and weightless. He would touch her everywhere and not hold anything back as they tried to find their way through each other to somewhere else.

Universal Girlfriend

Another Thursday night at the bar on Geary. Marianne drank beer with Jack while the others played foosball. Their shouts of profanity blended into the crowd: standing room only of rabid sports fans and misplaced tourists. March Madness, and all that it entailed, had begun.

On the television overhead, Stanford men's team played in the first round. Their lower-seed opponent was better than expected, making the bar rock with nervous laughter and empty taunts. When Stanford called a time-out, Jack twisted around to Marianne. He turned his hat backward and pushed up the sleeves of his well-worn sweatshirt.

"This could be it." He rubbed his hands together. "I can feel it."

"Would anything really change if they won?" Marianne sipped the last of her beer.

"Bragging rights. Respect for the program. I'd win the pool for once."

Marianne cradled her face in her hands, picturing all of them here again next year. Right now the air was filled with the belief that things could be different but Marianne knew better. Respect had nothing to do with it. She pushed her empty mug away and signaled to the waitress.

"Haven't you had enough?" Jack's smooth boy-next-door face turned sour. "I don't want to babysit you."

"Don't you worry about me," Marianne answered.

She turned to watch the guys behind her. Miguel, the best of the bunch, played alone on one side. Ox, his face red and sweaty, teamed with Rocky on the other. A shock of Rocky's red hair hung into his eyes, reminding Marianne of the Rhode Island Red chickens they had growing up. Marianne watched Rocky's fingers twitch on the yellow handles before slamming in a goal with a snap of his wrist. Chickens were uncomplicated, her mother liked to say.

"I want to play with Rocky," Marianne announced.

"Take my place," Ox said. "Should be watching the game anyway."

Marianne slid in beside Rocky, smelling his scent of dark beer and cigarettes. He brushed the hair from his eyes but it fell right back into place. Jack followed Marianne to the table, taking sides with Miguel.

The sounds and rhythm of the foosball game was punctuated by grunts from the boys and an occasional apology from Marianne. She tried to concentrate but Rocky kept shifting around next to her, jutting his hip into her now and then. On the last ball, the game was tied. Marianne accidentally let go of the handle and her men spun around the bar.

"No spins," Jack yelled as Rocky scored. Jack pounded his fist on the table. "How many times do I have to tell you?"

"Sorry," Marianne said.

Rocky patted her back. "Nice pass."

"How'd you get so good?" she asked.

"I put my whole body into it."

He leaned on the table and looked into Marianne's eyes. She felt a witty answer bubbling up but Jack spoke sharply to her.

"I thought you wanted another beer."

Jack held out his hand but Marianne walked past him toward their table. A fresh mug of lemony wheat beer—*that girly shit*, Ox called it—was waiting for her. On the television, there were four minutes left in the second half and Stanford led by three.

"You are definitely not drinking enough," Rocky said. He lifted the glass to Marianne's lips. She closed her eyes and gulped. It was all so familiar, the closeness of the bar, the boys, the beer.

"What's with you tonight?" Jack asked her.

He leaned into Marianne, smelling of Guinness, the smell of overcooked steak. When they started dating in college, Jack only drank local micro-brews. His wide body and easy smile had soothed her unfocused life. On their first date, he picked wild daisies for her in a field near Lake Merced. The smell of the dirt on his hands mixed with the sweetness of the flowers made her dizzy. From that day on, she painted her toenails, wore her sexiest underwear, and drank beer.

"Nothing." She pushed him away.

Cheers erupted and they looked up to watch the replay of tall, acned Casey Jacobson slide in a long three-pointer to put Stanford up by six. Ox traded high-fives with strangers while Rocky and Miguel pounded each other on the back. They all seemed to forget she had gone to Stanford, too. Ox sat down facing Marianne and stared hard for a minute.

"When are you setting me up with Sandy?" he shouted at her. "I gotta hit that."

"Becky," she said. "And never."

"What good are you then?" Ox turned to the television.

"Want to get something to eat?" Rocky asked her.

Marianne stared at the television, pretending not to hear him. Rocky and Jack had been friends before she met either of them.

"Marianne?" Rocky said louder.

She was about to answer when laughter broke into her thoughts. Marianne turned and saw two women at a nearby table. The women were drinking cocktails, oblivious to crowd of men and the game on the television. Marianne thought of her girlfriends from college, the ones she let slip away, replaced by Jack's pals. She strained to hear the women, wondering what they were talking about. Something other than shooting percentages and blocked shots.

Ox, shouting at the television, started pounding on the

table, making the beers spill over. They all looked up to see Mad Dog Madsen steal the ball and pass it to Casey, only one man between him and the basket. Casey leapt up and sunk another three-pointer to beat the no-name team, leading Stanford to the next round. Rocky repeated Marianne's name while Jack ordered more beer.

The next Saturday, at their usual table, Ox asked Marianne for help planning Memorial Day weekend at his parents' Lake Tahoe cabin. They went every year. Marianne loved the lake in the summer—the flowers during morning hikes, the cool lake water in the afternoons. She listened as Miguel talked about the hot tub and the girls he would invite, and promised herself that this year she would escape them all, even Jack, at least for a few hours.

Stanford was up by twelve at halftime, only twenty minutes from their first Final Four appearance in fifty years. Maybe things would change, Marianne thought as she watched Miguel beat Rocky at foosball. Rocky motioned her over but she shook her head. Ox ordered another Guinness and urged Marianne to try it. She refused, gripping her mug of wheat beer.

"Tell me about Sandy, again," Ox said and then belched. "You said she was hot."

"It's Becky. Let it go," she said.

Rocky and Miguel came back to the table as Stanford returned to the court. The crowd on television was a blur of red rally towels.

"Where's Jack?" Miguel asked.

Marianne shrugged. "All he said was change of plans."

"Goddammit I hate change," Ox said.

Rocky leaned across Marianne to grab his beer mug and for a moment, maybe it was the Guinness on his breath or the cologne he was wearing, he smelled just like Jack. All of them, staring at her as Rocky brushed her shoulder, seemed to smell exactly alike.

"What if Jack and I broke up?" Marianne said. "Things would change."

"You guys are breaking up?" Rocky asked. His hair looked like burnished copper under the glow of the bar lights.

"Even if you did break up," Miguel said, "you know we'll still be here."

Marianne tried to think of a contradiction while they stared at her, but looking from Rocky's red hair to Ox's thick eyebrows, nothing came to her. They all turned back to the game.

After three more rounds of beer and Stanford's lopsided victory, Marianne let Rocky guide her back home. She called out but Jack wasn't there.

As Rocky used the bathroom, Marianne stood on a chair in the kitchen to reach the cabinet above the stove. After pouring a jigger of whiskey, Marianne held her breath and shot it back. Still on the chair, she leaned forward to rest her cheek against the smooth wood cabinet. The curtains on the window over the sink were parted and it took a moment for Marianne to understand what she was seeing. In the darkness outside, just to the left of the buildings, were two yellowish balls of light. They were the tips of the Golden Gate Bridge, hovering detached, it seemed, in the fogless night. She never knew she could see that far from the apartment.

When she first moved to the city, Marianne would go to Fort Point below the bridge and listen to the ocean rush beneath it. The noise drowned out the sounds of cars above and the city behind her. It unsettled her at first, the unexpected voice of the water screaming against the rocks, but she grew accustomed to it, as she had to everything else.

The toilet flushed. Marianne stepped down from the chair as Rocky walked into the kitchen. Rocky lived alone, which Marianne couldn't comprehend. Sleeping alone made her nervous; waking up alone was even worse.

"Jack's not home?"

"Whiskey?" Marianne held up the bottle.

Rocky pulled Marianne to him. Up close, she noticed how much shorter he was than Jack. Not bad; just different. He kissed her. Though she was expecting it, Marianne found herself uninterested. His lips were warm; his breath strong and bitter. He reached under her blouse. This doesn't feel right either, Marianne thought. Wasn't there some kind of rule? She pushed him away.

"You have to go," she said.

"I thought things were happening."

She told him to leave.

"Is it about Jack?" he asked.

Marianne walked past him into the bedroom and lay on the bed fully dressed, facing away from the door. She felt Rocky watching her from the doorway. Finally, he snapped off the light and left.

The smells of the apartment were stronger in the dark: Jack's vinegary Rogaine shampoo in the shower, the sour smell of his gym bag, his leftover Chinese food. She didn't smell anything of hers.

Marianne awoke the next morning to the sound of Jack's snoring. He was flung out, taking up nearly all the bed, while she lay cramped against the wall. She peeked at the clock; it was just after nine. If she was late to soccer, Miguel would kill her. She thought about how compact and graceful Miguel was, how little room he would take up in bed. When Jack turned over, Marianne got up and searched in the closet for her gym bag.

"Great game, huh?" Jack's voice was thick, as if he'd been smoking.

"Where were you?" Marianne sat on the edge of the bed and pulled on her shin guards.

"Went out with some guys from work. Something different, you know?"

Marianne held her breath for a moment, feeling the blood pound in her temples. There was so much she could say. Jack reached for her.

"I'm gonna be late," she said.

"It's just a game."

"Miguel's counting on me."

Jack drummed his fingers against Marianne's thighs. "I can count on you, too."

He lifted the front of her shirt. "One, two…"

"Seriously," she said.

"What about me? I thought we could read the paper in bed."

Marianne turned away from his naked chest and bent down to tie her cleats, the taste of whiskey and beer rising up. If she never read the paper in bed with a man again, she wouldn't mind. There had to be something else to do on Sunday besides read the paper, watch sports or play soccer.

"You'll be fine on your own," she said.

The game had just begun when Marianne ran onto the field at 38th and Quintera. She first played soccer in college, before she met Jack, when Miguel invited her to a pick-up game. She improved over the years but knew her limitations. When the ball was kicked out of bounds, Marianne introduced herself to the new girl playing defense.

"Emily," the girl replied. "Friend of Miguel's."

"Of course."

Marianne looked over at Miguel, who was setting up a corner kick. They were together once, a long-ago night in college after a pickup game. They were happy and drunk, and in the morning she had mistakenly put on his long striped socks still crunchy with dirt. For days she had felt his strong, unfamiliar kisses on her body. They had never talked about it and it never happened again.

During the game, Marianne made three crucial mistakes, including a misdirected pass that led to an easy goal by the opponent. Miguel scowled at Marianne, who mouthed back, *It's just a game*. Miguel scored a late goal to bring them within one but time ran out. Playoffs were in two weeks and Marianne knew Miguel was annoyed.

"Ready?" Miguel smiled at Emily, his anger gone.

They had sex that morning, Marianne realized. She could tell by the way his eyes shone. He was probably itching to tell Marianne the details but she didn't want to hear them this time.

"See you next week," Emily said to Marianne as they turned to leave.

"Sure." She winked at Miguel.

He dropped his soccer bag, grabbed Marianne by the arm and pulled her away.

"What's with you?" he asked.

"Nothing," Marianne laughed, wrenching her arm free. "But it's like a revolving door with you."

"Who are you to judge my love life?"

She didn't answer. Emily watched them, shading her eyes against the sun. Marianne wanted to shout a warning to her but couldn't think of what to say.

"That's what I thought," Miguel said.

He jogged back to Emily, clumps of dirt and grass flying from his cleats. Marianne sometimes thought that if something ever happened with Jack, there would always be Miguel.

She zipped her bag and walked toward the bus stop. From that side of the field, she could just see the edge of the ocean disappearing into the sky. She often forgot that San Francisco was surrounded by water.

On Tuesday, Marianne headed to the bar after work. Ox was on his second beer.

"Where's Jack?" he asked when Marianne sat down.

"Don't know."

"Well, I need to talk to you anyway."

"Please. Not about Becky."

"I seriously need a girlfriend."

In the mirror over the back bar, Marianne looked at her and Ox's reflection. How was she there again, listening to Ox talk about what he would do when he got a girlfriend?

"You listening to me?" Ox tapped her on the forearm.

"Sure, go on."

It wasn't that Ox was unattractive, Marianne thought as he chattered on, he just scared women. He was big and loud and the drunker he got, the bigger and louder he became. He could be really funny, too. Usually she could tell the boys apart with her eyes closed, by their smells and their voices, but since March Madness began things were getting fuzzy. Tonight, Ox somehow sounded like Rocky and Jack combined.

As the night wore on, and they drank round after round, Ox grew less scary and Marianne wondered if someday she would date him, too.

On Saturday afternoon, Stanford played their Final Four game against Duke. The winner would play for the national championship. Marianne worked late but caught most of the game on the radio. Mad Dog had no signs of his injury and Casey hadn't missed a three all night. With ten minutes left in the second half, Marianne walked into the bar, the air heavy with anxiety. She wasn't sure what to expect. For the past few days, Rocky had been calling her and Marianne didn't know what to tell Jack. She started going to bed an hour early, enjoying the expanse of the bed around her.

The bar was packed and the boys weren't at their usual table. With a game this important, there would be no foosball. Making her way to the bar, Marianne ordered her beer then pushed through the crowd. She paused next to two women sitting on bar stools as they looked at photos, their shoulders hunched against the surge of men. One of the women looked up and smiled at Marianne, a bit of calm in the frenzy of voices. Marianne caught just a glimpse of the photos before the momentum of the crowd carried her forward.

The boys were sitting at the bar, their backs to her. As she stopped behind them, Marianne looked up at the television. A close-up of Casey on the big screen showed his dark hair freshly streaked blond and the faces of his teammates grim with determination. As she was about to touch Jack on the shoulder, Ox's voice rose above the others.

"Guess it'll be your turn next." Ox punched Rocky on the shoulder.

The boys leaned in together, as if plotting something. Images of a lonely farmhouse swept through Marianne's mind. She was in the kitchen cooking and keeping house for these three men, a half-dozen kids crawling around on the floor beneath her.

"I bet it'll be Miguel," Rocky said.

"You guys don't even know," Miguel said.

"Know what?"

"I already had my turn. Back in college."

"And?" Jack's voice was amused and not the least bit jealous.

"She's not my type," Miguel said. "Don't get me wrong, she's great and all."

"Too tomboyish," Ox said.

The crowd surged and Marianne looked up again. On the big screen, Mad Dog Madsen's red mouthpiece looked the size of a football and Marianne imagined she could smell his testosterone through the television.

"Not always a bad thing." That was Rocky.

Marianne wondered what her mother, with her endless supply of husbands, would do in a moment like this. No, Marianne decided, it was time for something else.

She glanced at the television just as Mad Dog intercepted a sloppy Duke pass. The crowd, in the bar and on the screen, held its breath. Mad Dog, grinning like a beast, ran alone down the court toward the unguarded basket. He looked behind him, mouthpiece flashing, before leaping into the air and dunking the ball into the basket as the final buzzer sounded, putting Stanford up for good by two points. Yes, Marianne thought, things could change.

There was a beat, before Mad Dog let go of the rim and floated back down to the floor, when no one in the bar understood just what had happened. That was the moment Marianne took a final long drink from the cold mug, filling herself with the womanly taste of yeast and lemon.

She stepped up to the bar between Rocky and Jack and hurled the empty mug at the television screen. Sparks and chunks of glass rained down and sweet smell of the beer was unleashed. The crowd hushed instantly, the only sound from the other televisions around the room. The boys turned to her, the cheers on their lips dying as gasps.

"What the hell!" Jack yelled.

"I'm breaking up with you," Marianne said in a strong voice.

"What are you talking about?" Rocky pulled her arm, looking from her face to Jack's and back.

"I'm breaking up with you!" Marianne stepped back, gesturing. "I'm breaking up with all of you!"

The crowd was shouting at her now, pressing in to her as the bartender climbed over the bar.

"I'm going to date myself for a while," Marianne yelled.

The broad-shouldered bouncer reached her first, wrapping his arm around her waist and lifting her off the ground. The crowd cheered as the man carried Marianne toward the front door. She didn't struggle. The boys gaped after her but none of them moved. They would never understand and she didn't care.

The bouncer shoved Marianne onto the sidewalk, where she stumbled but didn't fall. The door swung shut behind her. She stood still in the glow of the setting sun, panting.

THE SMALL OF HER BACK

A t the counter of the Flying J at the north end of Punxsutawney, Patrick motioned for a refill. A man came through the diner's door, bringing in a gust of frigid air that swept down Patrick's collar. The man took the seat next to him and nodded.

"Snowing yet?" Patrick asked.

"Not since Connecticut."

"Gonna be this cold," Patrick said, "might as well snow."

The man nodded again as Patrick pulled up his collar and closed his eyes. Images of sandy beaches competed with the hum of voices around him. The warm California sun, only a few days away, was just what he needed.

"Was it the meatloaf?" a voice asked.

Patrick opened his eyes to see the waitress—Judy, her nametag reminded him—refill his cup and remove his plate. He was about to close his eyes again when Judy turned around and bent over to set the plate in a bin.

Patrick had seen Judy before on this route. She was older than the other girls—late thirties, he guessed—and nothing about her seemed temporary. Her uniform was too snug, the buttons straining across her ample chest, but that wasn't what caught his eye. When she bent over, the space between the bottom of her blouse and the waistband of her skirt had widened, and there, on the small of her back, was a tattoo of a green, sleeping dragon.

It was the most surprising thing Patrick had seen in a long time. He started to say something but Judy lifted her head and caught his gaze in the mirror. He looked from the tattoo to her expectant blue eyes. She was waiting for him to say something. Something she heard from every other man who sat at that counter. Judy closed her eyes as if bracing herself. Before she opened them, Patrick backed away from the counter until the cold metal handle of the door hit his hip. He stepped outside, trying to conjure an image of the beach from the empty parking lot before him, but Judy's tattoo blocked it out.

She wasn't the type Patrick normally chatted up when he stopped for a bite. Definitely not the type he invited to a hotel room, which was exactly what he was considering. He should get into his truck and continue on to California to deliver the load of cheese. Then he could head to San Diego as planned.

Patrick watched his breath fade into the afternoon light. It should be snowing by now, he thought. When he looked through the diner window, Judy was watching him.

"Where is it?" Gail, the cheese buyer, shouted at the speaker-phone. She stood at her office window, working to get it open. In San Francisco, the morning was a clear fifty-six degrees. "That's why I'm calling."

Sal, a dispatcher at the trucking company, was simply a voice in Texas, one Gail heard only when there was bad news. The driver of her shipment had missed his status call. "He's not answering his phone." Sal was eating while he spoke. "Can't get 'em unless they answer their phones."

"I need that cheese," Gail said. "It's useless after Friday. You know what perishable means, don't you, Sal?"

"What do you want me to do?"

"I'm not fooling around."

"Keep your shirt on. You'll get your truck."

"It's the cheese I want, I don't give a fig about the truck."

After she hung up, Gail marched into the warehouse where her problem was just one of many. Earlier that week, a flood in Monterey had destroyed the micro-greens crop and a truck coming up from Mexico had blown a tire and dumped its load of chiles and spices.

Inside the walk-in, Gail nodded to the guys loading boxes and grabbed an inventory sheet. It was all written down but she wanted to see for herself. She ran her hands over the cold blocks of cheese. Some had been sitting for a while but it would have to do. Gail knew which chefs in town she could placate or bribe. She wasn't about to lose everything she'd built up during the last eight years over a hack driver who'd broken down somewhere in Pennsylvania.

It had taken more convincing than Patrick had been prepared for. Judy wasn't young and that — combined with her hesitation — made him more curious. He waited in his cab until her shift was over, ignoring the ring of his cell phone. While the heater blasted, he listened to a hockey game on the radio.

The phone stopped ringing, then began again. He knew it was Sal, whose company owned the truck, but he wasn't worried about Sal. It was the buyer, Gail, who was probably up in arms. When Judy stepped out of the diner, Patrick shoved the phone under the seat.

Inside the motel room, dusky light came in through the edges of the heavy curtains. Neither of them switched on the light. Patrick wasn't nervous as he moved toward Judy, not like he sometimes was with the young ones. Judy stood still until Patrick was right in front of her, then reached up and slipped her hand onto the back of his neck.

He came quickly, surprising them both. Patrick expected Judy to get dressed and leave, disappointed and ready to tell a tale, but she came back from the bathroom smiling. She curled naked against him, resting her slender hand on his chest. He felt his heart throb against her palm. They shared a cigarette and watched hockey on the muted television. Patrick stroked Judy's hair, letting the long strands slip through his fingers.

"I haven't done this in a long time, you know." Judy tapped his shoulder. "Don't look at me like that. You don't know me well enough to look at me like that. I swore to never get involved with a trucker again."

"You call this involved?"

She waved him off, the cigarette smoke curling around her fingers. "It's not a lifestyle for me," she said. "Some of the girls, a different guy every week, thinking each time he might be the one. As if Prince Charming would drive a truck."

"Don't think so, do you?"

She handed him the cigarette to finish and rested her head on his shoulder. They watched the game until Patrick saw her glance at the alarm clock on the nightstand. He lifted the sheet, pushed her gently onto her stomach and began to trace the tattoo with his fingertips.

"Tell me," he said.

She was seventeen, working the counter at Dairy Queen. Earlier that summer, her sister had fled to the city.

The only tattoo shop in town was in the strip mall behind Dairy Queen. One afternoon, Judy pressed her face against the window to see the drawings inside—skulls and snakes and lightning bolts. The door opened and a group of boys tumbled onto the sidewalk. They laughed at Judy, pointing at her pale legs. As Judy turned away, a girl came out and yelled at the boys. She looked at Judy as the boys took off.

"Come on." The girl held open the door. Judy glanced at the tattoo of daisies around her wrist. "You'll hate yourself if you don't."

Judy made herself a deal. If she didn't see any design she liked, she would leave. But as soon as she walked in, she saw it on the wall—a drawing of a sleeping dragon, wildly colored in red, yellow and orange. The cartoon was so big it would cover Judy's whole back. But, Judy thought, she could handle something smaller. And just one color wouldn't hurt so bad, she told herself, as the girl rummaged for tracing paper.

"How's this?" The girl held up the paper.

"Yes. Just green," Judy said. "My favorite color."

Behind a partition, Judy unbuttoned her jeans as the girl motioned toward an upholstered chair. Judy straddled the chair and bent forward. The air was cold on her exposed back as she watched the girl set up.

The first prick of the needle made Judy jump so high she hit her head on the shelf above, rattling glass jars of Q-tips and gauze. As Judy stood shaking, her back throbbing, she knew she couldn't bear the pain. But the girl didn't wait. She yanked Judy down, said "deep breath," and started in with the needle.

"Feels like it's happening to someone else," Judy whispered.

"Endorphins," the girl said.

In the mirror, Judy could see black ink mixed with blood on a piece of gauze in the girl's hand. The endorphins were fading and Judy could feel the pricking of her skin all over again. She dug her fingernails into the padding of the chair. Later at home, she would scrape bits of blue fabric from under her fingertips.

"Almost done with the outline," the girl said.

"That's the worst part, right?"

The girl smiled at Judy in the mirror. Green ink was smudged under her left eye.

"Sure," the girl answered.

The pain went in waves. Endorphins, Judy repeated to herself. Also this: if she could do this, she could do anything. Faith, Judy had always thought, had to do with God and miracles. But, she was beginning to understand, faith was simply the belief that something could be done. Courage was what you needed to do it.

At the one-hour mark, Judy thought she might faint. Her freckles had disappeared into the paleness of her face.

"It hurts," she whispered.

"Relax," the girl said.

After another five minutes, the girl sat back and snapped off her gloves. Judy collapsed against the chair. The girl dug into a jar of balm and rubbed some onto the fresh wound with a touch so tender it made Judy cry.

Gail watched out the window of her office at the branches of a tree moving in the breeze. She didn't know what kind of tree it was. Trivia like the names of trees or birds or solar systems were useless to Gail but today she wished she knew what kind of tree it was. The phone rang.

"His truck was spotted off a turnpike in northern Pennsylvania." Sal sighed. "Still not answering his phone."

"So if you know where he is, go get him."

"It's not that simple," Sal said. "Look, I can get you another driver for pickup day after tomorrow. Four days late is all."

"You think I can get cheese again just like that?"

"You're a smart gal, you'll think of something."

Gail slowly counted to ten.

"Still there, Gail?"

"I want to talk to that driver."

"Not gonna happen."

"But you know where he is?"

"Word is he's holed up with some waitress at a motel. Can't reach him. Didn't expect it from this one."

Gail thought about this. An adulterous affair, a drunken one-night stand, a Hollywood love-at-first-sight fling. Those she could grasp. Holed up was something new. To disappear from the world and forsake all responsibility. Not care that other people were counting on you. That was impossible.

"He doesn't expect to keep his job, does he?" she asked.

"Don't think he's worried about that right now. If you know what I mean."

"Someone should care, Sal. My job's in jeopardy, too."

"You're not going to lose your job over something you can't control."

"But I can control it." Gail hit the speakerphone button and walked to the window. She pictured Pennsylvania covered in snow. Quiet and peaceful—the way winters were supposed to be. "I order something, it comes in, I send it out. I control it all."

"Don't tell me in all these years something like this hasn't happened before."

"Not by some jerk probably left his wife for a piece of waitress ass—"

"So it's a morality thing?"

"I don't care what he does on his own time. That's my cheese."

"You're taking this way too personally. It's a great story. The guys here are dying."

"You're defending him?"

"Maybe you need to relax, let loose a bit."

Gail knocked the receiver from the stand, killing the line. She stared at the tree outside. How many times had she been told that? Lighten up, relax, give in to the moment. No one— not her son, not her mother, definitely not her ex-husband— had ever understood that this was living for her. This set rhythm of life, when things ran just as they should, that's what made it all work. Change meant chaos, and chaos meant not being able to count on anything.

Gail looked at the leaves on the trees, counted to ten, then called Sal back for the location of the truck.

When the phone rang, neither of them reached for it.

"Probably wrong number," Patrick mumbled.

The phone rang again. Patrick reached across Judy to pick it up.

"What?"

"This is Gail, the cheese buyer. Remember me?"

"Oh, hey." He sat up. "Sorry about your cheese."

There was silence. Patrick thought about hanging up but he was curious. From the little contact they had, he knew Gail was neurotic but he didn't think she would track him down. He slipped out of bed and walked naked to the window, stretching the phone cord to its limit.

"That's all you have to say?" Gail asked finally.

"If it's any consolation, I know I'm fired." He parted the heavy curtain with a finger, surprised to see two inches of snow on the ground. "Look at that, it's snowing."

Judy rolled over. "I thought I heard it snowing," she mumbled.

"What?" Patrick asked.

"Why?" Gail asked in his ear.

"Why is it snowing?" Patrick asked into the phone.

"Why are you doing this to me?" Gail asked.

Patrick felt the cold through the window, raising every

hair on his body. There was movement along the street but the sounds were muted by snow. When Gail repeated her question, Patrick moved to flip the heater on high, then returned to bed. He rested his hand on Judy's arm.

"Would you believe me if I told you I was in love?" Patrick said into the phone. He felt Judy shift under his fingers.

"No, I wouldn't," Gail said. "There's a difference between sex and love."

"There doesn't have to be."

"For men like you—"

"Don't finish that sentence, Gail." Judy's skin was warm under Patrick's palm. His fingers wandered across her body, down to where her back met the roundness of her hips. "You don't know me," he said. "Order your cheese again, they'll get someone to deliver it. Chalk it up to life and move on. There is no why for this."

At three in the afternoon, Patrick smoked in bed while Judy took a shower.

"What will you do?" Judy asked as she came naked into the room. She slipped into bed and ran her hands through Patrick's curly gray-brown chest hair.

"That's what this is all about, sweetie." He slid his hands along her body. "I usually just act. I finish a job, watch a ball game, go to sleep, get up the next day. Never stop to think about it. I'm forty-seven years old. Life isn't slowing down."

Judy said nothing, caught by the word *sweetie*. He didn't say it like the truckers at the diner who called her *honey* or *darling*. She believed he meant it, if only for that moment.

"Are you thinking about it?" Patrick said. "Losing your job?"

"I think too much," she said. "Not going to work is an action, right? Not acting is an act too, isn't it?"

"Some things just happen on their own."

They made love slowly, pausing after about twenty minutes, talking for a bit, then beginning again. Judy's own body surprised her. She hadn't enjoyed sex in a long time. It didn't happen often these days so it wasn't something she worried about. But this time was different. It felt so much better when she stopped wondering if he was enjoying himself. Of course he was.

Afterward, Judy could feel Patrick's breath slowing down toward sleep but her body still tingled. Forty-seven. He probably couldn't go again for a while. Less thinking, she told herself, more acting. She reached for his hand.

"More?" he asked.

"Yes."

"You're quite a gal."

"Don't think about it. Just do it."

"Turn over," he said.

It was a special trick, he told her. Something he learned from a girl who dated girls for a while. Judy did what he said and realized that, even at thirty-eight, she knew very little about the world.

"It's a rough time to travel, ma'am," the travel agent said. "Been snowing all day."

"I can drive there from the airport in three hours, right?" Gail sorted her inbox as the woman rattled off flight times over the speakerphone. It wasn't a good time to take time off work but there never was a good time.

"Yes, ma'am. Will you need a hotel?"

"No."

"Anything else? I can fax tips for driving in the snow."

"I grew up in Michigan," Gail snapped. "I think I remember how."

"Have a good time," Bill, her boss, told her as she said goodbye.

"I'm not going for fun."

"Do us all a favor and try."

Normally Gail would have spent a week arranging to leave but she only had time to get home and pack before driving to the airport. She wanted to catch Patrick before he left—to see what someone who could do this looked like. Then she'd visit the diner to see what woman would be taken in by that kind of man.

When Patrick woke up the next morning, he knew Judy would go back to work. She was asleep on her stomach, her face turned toward him. He lifted the sheet, bent over her back and softly kissed her tattoo.

She left without saying much. A quick shower, a lingering kiss and a slow drag on Patrick's cigarette. He knew she wouldn't regret it.

The phone rang ten minutes later. Patrick imagined it was Judy calling from the diner; the first sentimental thought he had in years. But it was Gail, on her way to the motel.

"If that's what you want, Gail, but can't promise I'll be here," he said.

"I don't care. I want that cheese."

"It's a long way to go to prove something."

"I've gone further."

"I'm sure you have."

"Just leave the truck keys at the motel office."

"But why?"

"That's none of your business. What about the girl?"

"She went back to work."

"Couldn't rescue her?"

"That wasn't the point."

"What was?"

Patrick lit a cigarette. Through the part in the curtains, he could see it was still snowing. He wondered if Gail had clothes for this kind of weather.

"Be careful driving," Patrick said and hung up.

He watched a game show while resting his hand on Judy's pillow. He pictured her bending over for silverware or a bottle of ketchup, her tattoo peeking out now and then.

Maybe he would wait for Gail to show up. Ask her if she had ever done anything that took blind courage.

SUPERGIRL

W ith her red cape fluttering around her shoulders, Janet sprinted west down California Street toward the glowing San Francisco sunset. Her honey-colored hair, set loose from its workday ponytail, streamed behind her like flames tailing off a rocket. For a moment, the pink and orange glow of the sun before her lit the world on fire.

As she crossed against the light, Janet noticed the crowd waiting at the intersection: a boy and girl holding hands, an old lady carrying a bag of groceries, a woman with a baby-stroller. They stared after her, but Janet knew none of them needed her help at the moment. Ahead, Janet saw a bus pulling up to the curb. She ran on, hearing only the sound of the heels of her new red boots striking the pavement.

Janet jumped onto the bottom step of the bus as the driver closed the door. As she dropped her money through the fare box, Janet looked down at her boots, surprised to discover that even after all that running, her feet didn't hurt a bit.

The red skirt and cape had been easy. Over the phone, Janet's mother talked her through cutting the fabric and sewing the hems. The blue leotard fit perfectly although the safety pins attaching the red and gold "S" to her chest scratched when she moved. She would get used to that.

She decided against a mask because in a city as congested as San Francisco, hiding her identity wasn't a problem. Days went by without someone looking directly at her as she shopped for groceries or sat on the bus. Everyone was busy: on the phone, rushing to work, waiting for a parking spot. If she were to walk down the street naked, people would just pretend they didn't see her. Supergirl, she thought, they'd notice.

The day before, she'd found the final element: tall, red boots. As soon as she stepped into the crowded downtown store at lunchtime, Janet saw the boots standing alone, high on a shelf. They were the only pair in the store: knee-high red leather lace-ups with eyes and hooks down the length of each boot. She had turned them over in her hands, feeling the stiff untouched leather. No size was marked but they looked like they would fit.

While lacing up the boots, Janet looked out the window at the people hurrying along the sidewalk and wondered if any of them felt like they had control over anything. When she had finished, Janet leapt around the store to make sure that they fit. And they did; as if they had been made just for her.

Janet wore them back to the office that day to break them in, handing her tattered slip-ons to a homeless woman petting a cat on the corner of Kearny and Sutter.

From deep within the bus, Janet watched the blanket of darkness fold over the city. Another mild and clear October night—Halloween. The boots made her feel strong and the skirt swayed pleasurably against her body from the motion of the bus. She thought, just for a moment, that she would miss the city if she moved back to her mother's house in Lodi.

The mood on the bus was loud and jovial with an undercurrent of mayhem, as if it was a private party bus and not the municipal system so hated by these same residents every other day of the year. Janet pulled the cape around her, trying not to get crushed by the other creatures: vampires, maids, grim reapers and fairy tale characters. Sprinkled among them were beings that may or may not have been wearing costumes.

When the bus reached the Castro district, the festivities were already in full swing. As Janet descended to the street, a voice on the sidewalk shouted at her.

"Save me, Supergirl!"

Someone else pulled one of Janet's ponytails.

"I'm dying!" a man laughed at her, spilling his drink on her tights.

With the cape draped around her shoulders, Janet moved through the cacophony of music and laughter on Castro Street. She watched the jumping action around her, her senses heightened with the weight of vigilance. A man clad only in leather chaps hung from a tree to the applause of people below. Drag queens in wild geisha costumes teetered by wearing towering wooden shoes. A woman dressed simply in jeans and a T-shirt sidled up to a ringmaster and asked to hold his whip. These were not problems.

Janet gravitated toward the dark alleys and side streets from where, by the end of the night, she had pulled a drunken Little Bo Peep out from under a malicious Tooth Fairy, reunited Fred Flintstone with his, or someone's, Wilma, and freed an androgynous pixie from an overturned Port-a-Potty.

Janet patrolled the streets until nearly two in the morning, when there was no one left and she was no longer needed. While waiting for the bus near Walgreen's, Janet watched two nurses stumble along the sidewalk, talking about turning milk into pudding. A few minutes later, a geisha lurched by peering down into the trash-strewn gutter. The geisha, who was at least a foot taller than Janet, wore only one shoe and a flowing white robe edged in gold with a pink silk sash across the high waist. Janet would have to tell her mother about such an outfit. The geisha stopped next to Janet.

"Nice costume," the geisha said. Only by his voice could Janet tell it was a man. "And those boots. Yummy."

Janet smiled, pulled her cape around her, then turned back to the nurses.

"Will you help me find my shoe?" The geisha touched the hem of her cape.

"Where did you last see it?" Janet gazed up into the geisha's thickly painted face and let him stroke the cape. His mascara had run into wide black circles beneath his eyes and one false eyelash hung by an edge. Janet wanted to touch his brown, glossy wig held in a tall topknot with chopsticks, but she couldn't reach that high. The geisha gestured to the empty intersection.

"Somewhere in the Castro," he answered.

"That might be difficult," she said.

"But you're Supergirl." The geisha squinted into Janet's face. "Hey, I know you."

"I don't think so." Janet turned away and squinted up the sidewalk. The nurses had stopped about ten feet away and the shorter one was attempting to lay down in the gutter.

"Yes, yes." The geisha began jumping up and down, his shoe making a single clomp on the asphalt. "I work at Peet's downtown. You come in every day about ten o'clock for a double skim latte. Sometimes a shot of vanilla. I don't know your name, but I know you. What's your name?"

"Supergirl." Janet tried to remember if she had seen him before. Normally, she didn't look too closely at people.

"I am Annabella." He bent deep at the waist.

"Is that a real geisha name?" Janet held his arm as he straightened up.

"Pretty, isn't it?"

"I have to go," she said.

Up the street, the tall nurse pulled the other one to her feet and they were heading into the Walgreen's. A man in a Raiders uniform appeared out of nowhere and followed the nurses inside.

"Forget the shoe." The geisha took Janet's hand again. "Let's have a drink. It's just sad...all dressed up and nowhere to go."

"Everything's closed. They've all gone home."

"Come to Chez Maurice then." He tried to whisper. "That's my real name."

"But the nurses..."

"They'll be fine." The geisha gestured to the bus pulling

up in front of Walgreen's. The nurses rushed from the store and into the back of the cab as the Raider stumbled out, shaking his fist after them.

Janet followed Maurice down an alley off 14th Street and up to his third-floor apartment.

"You'll love it, I promise," he said as they climbed the stairs.

Inside, Maurice took Janet to the living room, where a chest-high armoire towered like a gargoyle over the room's more sedate furnishings. The armoire was creamy white with gray, distressed seams and antique handles. Ornate frames holding black and white photos dotted the shiny top, which was encircled by a small guardrail.

"It's beautiful," Janet said, not sure what he wanted from her.

"Ah, but it is what's inside that counts, right?"

Maurice threw open the doors to reveal the unexpected: rather than shelves for a stereo or television, the armoire was a wet bar. There were drawers for mixers and spirits, a small freezer with miniature ice trays, a cabinet for glassware, and rows of wine bottles.

"I owe everything to HGTV." Maurice gestured around the room.

"Just water, thanks."

While Maurice clomped into the kitchen, Janet looked at the photos on top of the armoire. An older woman, who closely resembled Maurice as a geisha, stood in front of a cake decorated with frosted ladybugs. An older man sat astride a lawn mower wearing a hunting hat with the flaps down. Another photo showed a family picnic near a lake. Maurice, skinny in a black long-sleeve shirt and black jeans, stood slightly apart from his overgrown, pastel family. It could have been anyone's family. Maurice, handing Janet a glass of water, laid a thick finger over the faces of the couple near the head of the front table.

"My parents. As the Lord said, the hicks will inherit the earth."

Maurice used a white dish towel to wipe his face, removing some, but not all, of the thick makeup. Then he pulled off the wig and stepped out of his remaining shoe.

He was bald, with just a shadow of hair around the sides of his head, and lost nearly four inches in stocking feet. Even with the makeup streaked across his face, he looked quite ordinary, like someone Janet would know.

"Shall we drink al fresco?" he asked.

He poured a highball glass of whiskey and added a handful of mini ice cubes. He threw the towel into a compartment of the wet bar and closed the door while Janet combed his wig with her fingers.

"Are you coming?" he called over his shoulder.

Janet nodded, letting the curly tendrils of the wig bounce back into place. As Maurice held open the back door, Janet felt her way up the dark staircase. It occurred to her then, the only time she would have the thought, that she didn't know this man. That no one knew where she was. No one ever knew where she was.

"Love those boots." Maurice's face was at her feet as she ascended ahead of him. "I can never find the good stuff in my size."

"Try Discount Pavilion on Kearny," Janet replied. "They have plenty of large sizes there."

"Maybe we can go shopping sometime." He gave Janet a nudge at the top of the stairs.

Janet stumbled onto the flat, gravelly roof. The edge was closer than she expected so she took a step back, bumping against Maurice. There was no rail around the perimeter of the roof; it just dropped off. Maurice grabbed Janet's arm.

"You're fine," he said.

He stepped around Janet and sat down at the roof's edge, letting his long legs dangle off as if he were sitting at a lakeside pier.

"Don't tell me Supergirl's afraid of heights?"

"Just of falling." Janet inched closer to him.

"Come on." Maurice held out his hand. "I got you."

Janet grasped his hand. They remained like that for a moment as Janet soaked in the view. It wasn't just that the lights made the city beautiful; it was their irregularity. The hills and the trees made odd juxtapositions of light and dark across the landscape so it was hard to tell where she was, if she was even in San Francisco at that moment.

Janet moved her hand to Maurice's shoulder and he grasped her around the boots. She sank down next to him but didn't dare dangle her feet.

"My family's all in Fresno," Maurice said quietly. "Been there since before I was born. Can't understand why I wanted to move to a big scary city." He mocked a woman's shrill voice. "It's so expensive, the crime. AIDS, Maury, AIDS." He shifted and a few pebbles fell over the side. Janet heard the faint sound of the stones hitting an awning below. "You know the only difference between falling and jumping is a matter of control, right?" he asked Janet. "Either you have it or you don't."

Janet nodded. She'd driven through Fresno once on the way to Los Angeles. It hadn't been all that different from Lodi, where she had grown up and was thinking of returning. At that moment, it was difficult to imagine Maurice, or herself, anywhere but on a roof in the middle of San Francisco.

"I'm happy they have their thing," Maurice continued. "But I needed to find mine. They can't understand that."

"And have you?"

"Not yet," he said.

A voice boomed behind them, making Janet nearly pitch over the edge. Maurice grabbed her arm and laughed.

"I figured he'd show up sooner or later." Maurice stood up, pulling Janet to her feet. "That," he said, gesturing, "is Reese."

"Hello, all."

Reese, dressed as a Viking with long blond hair, breastplate and gold-horned hat, was a six-foot-five sparkling vision of gold in the moonlight. Janet pictured him dressed like that riding the bus to work or ordering coffee at Peet's, his breastplate glimmering in the morning light. He looked, Janet thought, just as he should.

"There are two kinds of people in the world," Reese announced. He held out a bundle, which Maurice stepped forward to accept. "Those that want to dress up every day," he indicated the three of them with a sweep of his arm, "and those that do it on Halloween out of some sense of duty. I think, hello, darling," he accepted a kiss from Maurice, "that if you don't believe in something one hundred percent, you shouldn't do it at all." He squinted at Janet who was unsure whether to bolt down the stairs or simply stare at the beautiful man. "Who are you?"

"I'm Supergirl," Janet said.

"Of course you are." Reese nodded to Maurice, who unwrapped the bundle to reveal his lost wooden shoe. "I found it outside Moby Dick's," Reese said, "but I won't ask questions. Halloween is amnesty day, right?"

Maurice, grinning at Reese, made a sound in the back of his throat.

"Thanks for the view," Janet murmured.

Maurice didn't seem to hear. He had nestled up against Reese's gold-plated chest. Reese kissed his forehead. As Janet walked toward the stairs, Maurice reached out and stroked one of her ponytails.

"See you around, Supergirl," he said.

Sounds of kissing followed Janet as she crept down the stairs toward home.

Thirty minutes later, unable to find a cab, Janet was riding the bus. She was tired, but, like an animal, her ears pricked up at the low wail of a siren. Janet yanked the signal cord just as the bus screeched to a halt to let three fire trucks rush through the intersection. Ignoring the driver's protests, Janet jumped off the bus in the middle of the street.

She ran in the gutter along California Street, her legs growing heavy as she neared her neighborhood. Turning her street corner, she was filled with relief, then guilt, at seeing it was not her building on fire but the blue one across the street. Janet's landlady, Shirley, stood on the steps of their ugly pink house clutching her bathrobe and shouting in Chinese to no one in particular.

Small flames licked at the roof from the upper floor windows. The flames were brilliant against the sky but Janet knew she shouldn't think they were pretty. Four firefighters grappled with a live hose, directing it toward the roof. The front of the house and the sidewalks below were drenched with water. People milled about the street in bathrobes and pajamas. It was too late for costumes.

"What happened?" Janet asked a firefighter standing in the street.

"You live here?" He looked at Janet's boots and cape, then at the house. "There was nobody home. Just a simple fire in the front room. It'll be out soon."

"There was an old man." Janet pointed up. "He sat in the top window and watched the street."

"Neighbor said they were all on vacation," the firefighter said.

When Janet didn't answer, the man grabbed at the walkie-talkie on his shoulder, keeping his eyes on Janet's face.

"Anyone get an old man out?" he yelled.

Janet stood next to him, feeling the heat of the fire and the cold spray of water. Every few minutes someone yelled at her to get back.

"They'll check it out." The firefighter placed his hand on Janet's shoulder. "There's nothing you can do."

Janet backed away from him, thinking of home. Of her apartment, not her mother's home, not Lodi. She'd been in the city for three years, like a drop of oil in a bucket of water, unable to mix.

When the fireman moved away, Janet ducked behind the fire truck parked in front of the driveway. If the layout of that house was like hers, then the bedroom in the old man's apartment was at the back. Janet was soaked by the water from the hoses by the time she reached the breezeway door. She ran down the dark corridor and was halfway up the back steps when two firefighters shouted at her.

"I'm sure the old man's in there," Janet yelled back. "This leads to the kitchen."

The male firefighter, followed by the woman, raced up the steps past Janet, forcing her against the railing.

"Are you that stupid?" The man forced open the door with his shoulder.

The woman looked at Janet's wet cape and boots, and smiled. She had bright blue eyes and a square face.

"We've got it from here," she told Janet.

Janet nodded and walked down the stairs into the backyard. She sat on the damp lawn and pulled the cape tight around her shoulders, watching the firefighters move around the bedroom. Soon they emerged, carrying the old man down the stairs. There were no more flames against the night sky but Janet sat patiently in the grass. She would wait until all the trucks left before she went home.

Monday morning, Janet wore most of the costume under her work clothes. The tights felt smooth on her legs under her pants and she liked the crinkling sound the 'S' made when she moved. She was getting used to the rubbing of the safety pins on the leotard. The boots, which she would wear every day from then on, were a big hit with the other office assistants, who had never really spoken to her before. They buzzed around her now, asking where she bought the boots, their attention like a warm bath after walking in cold rain.

At ten o'clock, Janet worked up the courage to see Maurice. She was nervous that he would recognize her and even more afraid that he wouldn't. At Peet's, she stood in the long line watching Maurice work the espresso machine, calling out names in his booming voice. The coffee shop was crowded; Janet felt sweat forming at the waistband of her tights.

Finally at the counter, Janet ordered her double skim latte with a shot of vanilla and waited near the window. Through the glass, she thought she recognized another assistant from her office but didn't wave hello. When Maurice read Janet's order from the monitor, he lifted his head and looked around until he saw her. He beckoned her to the counter, where he pulled up his pant legs to reveal the wooden geisha shoes.

"They're actually quite comfortable," he said as he handed over her drink. "Come on, it's time for my break."

They walked through the side entrance into the alley. Maurice stepped off the curb so he wouldn't tower over Janet so much and lit a cigarette. They watched the office workers move past them along the sidewalk.

"I don't want to be cliché, you know?" Maurice said. "But

I don't want to be like my parents either." He sighed. "It's all just temporary, anyway. You understand, right?"

"You work every day?" Janet asked.

"Until three. Except Sundays. But I won't tell you what I do on Sundays."

"I won't ask." She smiled at him.

"You have a nice smile," he said. "And you know how I feel about those boots. The boys must go crazy."

Janet looked down. She wanted to talk to him about boys but didn't feel quite ready.

"Can I borrow your wig sometime?" she asked.

"Supergirl goes brunette?" Maurice dropped his cigarette in the gutter and stepped on it. "Anytime."

That night at her apartment, after she had taken off the boots and begun to brush her teeth, Janet heard the faint cry of a siren. She listened carefully while rinsing the toothpaste from her mouth. Soon the single siren was joined by others. They were coming closer. Janet stood in the middle of the living room, listening to the world around her. She was still wearing the tights and leotard. The 'S' on the chest was a beginning to curl at the edges. She would have to make a new one soon.

Janet put on her skirt and pulled the cape from the closet. The fire engines screamed along California Street heading west. Janet thought about all the people in the city she didn't know and, for the first time, thought she might like to know some of them. She sat down in the middle of her apartment, pulled on her shiny red boots and began to lace them up.

EARTHQUAKE WEATHER

I t wasn't just me. October 17, 1989, was burned into the collective consciousness of Northern California in a matter of seconds. I was at the beginning of a piano lesson with Brian Wu, a third-year student of immense talent and sloppy habits, when it happened.

Often I gave up correcting Brian and stared out the front window, simply listening to how he played. There was an ethereal quality in the careless way he played, as if he didn't notice his own hands. It was this lack of care that gave his music life. He didn't merely play the notes—I used to do that—but rather seduced meaning from the music.

The initial jolt of the quake was swift and violent, then smoothed into smaller waves. Brian jumped up from the bench and grabbed my arm, his nails biting into my skin. Together we moved to the kitchen doorway.

My cigarette and ashtray fell from the arm of the couch to the floor. The blinds swayed and rattled against the windows and the clock in the kitchen stopped at 5:04. A brass candlestick fell from the top of the piano and smashed three white keys and a black one. By the time I reached the burning cigarette, the house was calm again. It was then that I noticed how still the air was. The leaves of the trees outside weren't moving and the day was too warm for October. Earthquake weather.

We were sixty-three miles northeast of the epicenter yet it felt as if it was directly beneath me. When the aftershocks abated, I made Brian help me check the house. He was skittish and wouldn't go into the garage, so I sent him home. Only when I was alone sweeping up broken glass in the kitchen did I shake with fear.

In the weeks following the quake, I read and collected everything I could about those that died. The mother and baby trapped under their collapsed Marina District home. The woman driving on the top deck of the Bay Bridge as it cracked opened underneath her. I pored over the heroics of everyday citizens and joined a victim support group. Brian didn't return for lessons, which was just as well, as I couldn't bear his clammy hands running over the damaged piano.

I dragged my friend Franny to the fault site at Loma Prieta near Santa Cruz. She waited off to the side, panting from the hike up, as I traced the jagged grass growing up the mountain like a scar.

Other quakes struck in Japan, Turkey and Greece. They came in bunches, or only during the day, or only on minor faults. I watched the news, read books and kept notes, trying to find similarities in all the different incidents.

A month after the quake, my tenant—a sophomore music student at Berkeley named Abigail—moved out. Her parents, a sensible Ohio couple, decided tornadoes were less frightening than earthquakes and insisted she moved back home. Abigail had lived with me since her freshman year and, after a month of loneliness, I began interviewing replacements.

The most promising prospect was Laurie, a sophomore studying art history who wanted out of the dorms. She perched on the edge of the armchair, tapping her foot to the Schubert concerto on the stereo. I was smoking and telling her about how the earthquake damaged the piano, when something in her damp, babyish face caught my attention. There was an odd familiarity in her polite blue eyes, in the lids that drooped at the corners.

"What was your last name again?" I asked.

"Zambrosky."

"That's right." I exhaled smoke. "Unique name. Did I tell you, I received my music degree from Santa Barbara?"

"I'm from San Luis Obispo."

"Too far north, I guess."

"No offense." Laurie rose abruptly, her sneakers making indentations in the carpet. "Can I have the room or not?"

"Ever been in an earthquake?" I stamped out my cigarette.

"A few."

As she looked away, trying to hide her annoyance, I studied her face. She was nothing like the docile Abigail, but I was curious.

"Move in whenever you want," I said. "The room's all ready. We'll have the fire and earthquake drill in a couple weeks."

"A what?" She waved her hand at me. "Whatever." She hurried out the door, her blond ponytail disappearing from sight.

"Zamboni, Zambrosky," I muttered, moving to the kitchen to make a fresh cup of tea. "About the right age."

It was possible. Paul Zambrosky had a daughter, a pale blond slip of a thing when I first saw her more than a dozen years earlier. If this was her, she had grown up healthy and intact; no visible scars. Today her face had been confident with the smoothness of youth. It would be ten years before that began to fade

I hadn't thought about Paul in years, but it could be her. The last day I had seen Paul, a hot May afternoon, was the only time I'd seen his daughter. She was just five then, staring at the two of us in the dry heat of the Santa Barbara hills while I tried to tell him my theory about earthquake weather.

By June of that year, I finished my graduate studies, and left Santa Barbara and Paul behind. I followed the San Andreas Fault north to Berkeley, where I found the Shaw house. On my first visit with Mrs. Shaw, I followed her impatiently through the rooms, just as Laurie had done with me. Mrs. Shaw growled at me that she normally rented to students, not teachers, but when I sat down at the mahogany piano in the living room and played for an hour, she relented.

I taught music at the university and, sooner than I imagined, all the playing destroyed my hands. That's when I began to study earthquakes in earnest, trying to piece together theories about when they occurred and how to predict them. Gradually, earthquakes began to crowd out thoughts of Paul. I discovered the earthquake notations in the weather section of the newspaper. The earth moved every single day and I had never noticed it.

When Mrs. Shaw died, five years after I moved in, her oldest son stood in the living room surrounded by photos of his parents and asked if I wanted to buy the house. I was twenty-seven and thought it would be a good place to wait for my future.

When the doorbell rang at three o'clock, I opened the door just enough to tell an Indian woman that the room was taken. I taped a sign to the door and headed to the garage. I found the old shoebox marked "Paul" and took it upstairs.

I turned over the shoebox and dumped everything—shells, letters and photographs—onto my bedspread. Paul's letters and poems were tied together with faded ribbon. In each photo, Paul was alone. I remember—at the beach, a hotel pool—there was never anyone to take our photo together. I wondered if he had kept any photos of me. I took the photos to the bookshelf, propping them up against the dusty books.

I lit another cigarette and spent the fading afternoon hours looking through the box and thinking about Laurie Zambrosky.

The day Laurie moved in, a six-point-eight earthquake struck Mexico. Up early to make sweet rolls, I heard it on the news. Hundreds were dead, thousands injured, people buried alive under the rubble.

The kneading hurt my hands but I took a pill and kept going. There was nothing better than homemade sweet rolls. Laurie would smell them and know she made the right choice. Maybe her father—Paul—would come, too, carrying her boxes up the stairs. He wouldn't notice me until Laurie introduced us. Then he would smile and hold out his hand to me.

That afternoon in the hills, I followed them along the horse trail, far enough back that Paul didn't see me. They rode together on one horse; Paul holding the bridle with his daughter tucked in front of him. Suddenly the girl cried out and Paul jumped off the horse. I raced up to them as he examined her arm.

"Let me see." I got off my horse and grasped at her arm. A small patch of skin was turning red.

"What are you doing here!" Paul pulled her arm from me. "You aren't supposed to be here."

For a year before that last day, Paul told me repeatedly, *Don't worry. Nothing to get hysterical about.* His marriage and child were just things to be worked out, like kinks in a garden hose. But in that moment when I touched his little girl, everything changed. I spilled into his real life. It was no longer me—*my true love,* he told me—standing there on the dirt trail. I didn't exist beside his daughter; we couldn't exist in the same space.

"She's not having a reaction," I said. "It'll just hurt."

"You need to leave," he said. The girl had stopped crying and was staring at me.

"You haven't called in three days," I said.

"We are not having this conversation."

"We can talk about anything you want. What about the weather? Feel how still the air is?"

"Get out of here." He climbed back on the horse.

A group of riders passed along the trail, turning to stare at us.

"The air's always tight like this when we're about to have an earthquake," I said.

"I don't think so." He turned the horse away. The girl stared at me over her shoulder as Paul led the horse down the trail.

Now here she was—I was sure it was her. Once her friends finished carrying boxes up the stairs, the house was quiet again except for muffled sounds from her room. I went upstairs with a plate of sweet rolls.

Laurie was bent over a box, close enough that I could see the creamy skin of her arms.

I lingered in the doorway of her room and saw picture frames stacked on a light blue dresser.

"Do you need any help?"

"No, thanks," she said.

I set the plate on her dresser and went back to my room. I turned the radio to the news station—now two hundred dead in Mexico—and opened the window. The breeze was moist from the rain.

On her rental agreement, Laurie listed her home address in San Luis Obispo and her emergency contact was a brother named Seth in Sonoma. I didn't remember another child; he must have come later. I bribed her with what had worked on Abigail—elaborate dinners, homemade sweets and free piano lessons. Anything to get her to spend time with me. I thought I was getting somewhere but the night before another vigil, while getting ready for bed, I overheard Laurie on the phone.

"I keep telling myself, 'the rent is cheap, the rent is cheap,' whenever she starts in on me." She paused, then laughed. "She has books all over the place. *Sooner Than You Think: The Big One.* How about, *101 Ways to Safeguard Your House* or *What to Expect During the Big One.* She leaves her bedroom door wide open. As if I'd want to go in there." She laughed again. "I'm telling you, she's obsessed."

I turned up the radio and stared at the photos of Paul on the bookshelf. A few minutes later, Laurie knocked on my open door, staring at her feet.

"I'm going home tomorrow morning," she said. "I'll be back late."

"I thought you were going with me to the vigil?" I motioned her inside but she stayed in the doorway. "And we were going to have the drill."

"Something came up. Take Franny to the vigil."

"Is everything okay?" I reached out toward her.

"Don't worry. Just family stuff. You know how it is. Nothing to get hysterical about."

I stopped dead, my hands reaching out. *Could it just be a coincidence*, I thought, *her using that phrase?*

She yawned and rubbed one foot against the other. I stepped away from the bookshelf so she could see the photos but she looked back toward the hallway.

"Actually," I said. "I don't have much family. Did I tell you that?"

She shook her head and vanished before I could say anything else.

The next day, I stood alone in the dry dusk at Justin Herman Plaza in downtown San Francisco. Light lingered from the west; it was the final days of daylight savings. Marcella Nunez, whose mother died when the ceiling of a video store collapsed on her, was sobbing in the arms of another woman from our support group.

The moment of silence lasted sixty-three seconds. I tried to pray for each victim but my thoughts kept flying to Laurie and our earthquake drill. We were just begging for something to happen.

9:07 p.m., December 26. The moment I stepped out of the shower, the room began to slip. A few seconds later, everything was still again. Normally, I would have turned on the television but I had to hurry. Laurie would be back by ten.

Inside her room, I stood before her dresser. There was a pair of chopsticks strewn among the barrettes and perfume bottles. I pulled my wet hair into a bun and stuck a red chopstick through it. Then I peered closely at the framed photos on the wall.

There was Paul, his whole face staring out at me. I couldn't be positive but it felt like him. His hair was grayer but the eyes were the same robin blue. I picked up the next frame. In the photo a young girl stood in a plastic wading pool holding the same man's hand. He sat in a lawn chair, feet in the pool, shading his eyes from the sun. The girl was blond with nothing definite about her features yet.

I went to the closet and pushed back the clothes to reach the wall. After Loma Prieta, there'd been a superficial crack down the back wall side but I couldn't find any trace. I must have painted over it. It was hard to remember everything that had happened.

I leaned into Laurie's clothes, sniffing, hoping to find some scent of Paul but there was only the smell of fresh soap. All around me, I could feel Laurie's vitality, the energy that oozed from her youthfulness.

Hearing no sound in the house, I lay down on Laurie's bed and ran my hands along the green bedspread. Maybe Paul had helped her pick it out when she left for college. If things had shifted a different way, it could have been me.

Downstairs, the side door creaked. I closed her door just as Laurie reached the landing. Before she looked up, I yanked the chopstick from my hair and shoved it into my nightgown pocket. Laurie said hello then disappeared into the bathroom.

At eleven, Laurie sat in the armchair filing her nails and watching the news with me. I smoked on the couch, questions about her holiday at home hovering on my lips. The television showed a woman sweeping up broken bottles inside a store on Main Street in Bolinas, a one-stoplight town forty miles north. The earthquake had been a three-point-four. No injuries and no major damage.

"During the big one," I said, "you wouldn't believe how well people worked together. The Marina District was on fire, the bridge collapsed, freeways fell down. But all the emergency preparedness worked like clockwork. Just goes to show we can't be too prepared."

Laurie didn't look up from her nails.

"Where were you when it happened?" I asked.

"Home. We watched it on the news."

"Didn't you feel it?"

"No."

"What?" I pointed at the television. "People felt it up and down the entire Pacific coast. Alaska even. There were reports from Mexico. I don't think there was a single person in the state that didn't feel it."

Laurie looked at me sideways. "That was the day my dad moved out," she said flatly, blowing on her nails. "So, no, I didn't feel a thing."

I fingered the smooth chopstick in my pocket, wanting to hand it to her and confess. But there was a tightness to her lips that suggested any sudden movement would make her flee and never come back.

The earthquake hit at 5:43 a.m. Light was just breaking over the eastern hills as I stumbled to the landing with my flashlight. I pounded on Laurie's door. When she didn't answer, I opened it. By then the shaking had stopped. She was sound asleep, the comforter strewn sideways over her body, her hair swept across her face.

"Laurie! Wake up!"

"What is it?" she mumbled.

"How can you sleep?"

"What?" She sat up and pulled up the covers. "Get out of here!"

"How can you sleep? It was at least a five point zero." I pointed to her desk. A pile of books had fallen to the floor. "You should be under the desk."

"It's no big deal. They happen all the time." She narrowed her eyes, focusing on my nightgown. "You took my chopstick."

I grasped at the front of my nightgown. The red chopstick was sticking out of the pocket.

"I didn't mean to."

"You have no right to snoop." She jumped out of bed and grabbed the chopstick from me.

"I just wanted to see the photos," I stammered. "I think I knew your father."

Her eyes narrowed against the sharp morning light. I should have known it was coming. All week it had been seventy degrees with no wind off the bay, unusual for that time of year. I was already sweating.

"I don't think so," she said.

I grabbed her arm and looked closely at it. She pulled away, still scowling, but not before I saw that there was no mark, no scar, no sign at all. I grabbed her other arm. There was nothing there either.

"Don't touch me." She backed up to her bed.

"In Santa Barbara," I said. "I knew him."

"I don't even know my father." Her voice went soft. "He sends me things from Phoenix. Calls me on Christmas. I mean, anything's possible, right? But I doubt it."

"Did you ever go horseback riding with him?"

She exhaled, her face a mixture of anger and pity. "Please, just stay out of my room."

She handed me the chopstick and pushed me out the door, slamming it behind me. I stood in the hallway fingering the smooth, tapered wood and listening to the bed creak as Laurie settled back in.

What We Call Living

We are about an hour away. Soon we will be out of the car and back to our lives and faithful spouses, where we can pretend nothing has happened. But trapped behind a tanker truck, the trip is slow on the two-lane road. The sky is bleached with thin clouds and the sun plays hide-and-seek. I can't get comfortable in the seat. We haven't spoken for miles.

"Wish there was more than one way out of here," he says finally.

He is familiar with this part of the country. The houses are miles apart with long dirt driveways connecting them to the main road. There's an occasional pasture of cows. I can smell grass and manure even with the windows closed.

"It was cold when we left." I pull at the long sleeves of my shirt, jerking the material above my elbows. "I can't get used to this weather."

"Take it off then," he says.

I glance at him but he is not looking at me. He watches the road, the truck churning up the slight grade ahead. His eyes dart around to survey the options. I am surprised at his agitation. Until now he has been the calm one.

"I won't look," he says. "I promise."

"It's like wearing a bikini top."

"Exactly. Like Victoria's Secret. I look at those all the time. My wife doesn't mind."

I look up when he says the word "wife" but he doesn't turn his head. I stare at the truck ahead of us. I can't see the side mirrors, which means the driver can't see me. I take off my shirt and drape it across my lap.

The sun warms my skin through the window. He drives on, not looking.

We stop for gas. From inside the car I watch streaks of lightning play off to the left followed by thunder that sounds fake. I've never seen anything like this. The thunderstorms where I live are less dramatic. I lift the disposable camera to my eye.

"You can't do it," he says as we begin to drive again. "Photographers leave their shutters open all day to catch it. You think you can do it with cardboard?"

I want to argue. Surely I had taken a photo of lightning before. Why else would I be so certain now? I set the camera down and lean back in my seat.

It begins to rain, then harder. I laugh. When it turns to hail the size of lemons, I stop laughing. He drives on. A thick bolt of lightning strikes overhead.

"You okay?" he asks.

"Nervous," I whisper.

"Do you want me to pull over?"

I shake my head. There are cars, trucks and minivans strewn on the side of the highway, their blinkers dim in the torrent of water. I can't tell if there's been an accident or if they are just afraid, like me. I don't want to be with them.

"May I touch you?" I ask.

"To be grounded?" He tries to laugh.

I rest my hand on his shoulder. "Is that good or bad?"

He smiles and gently pumps the brakes.

We've driven three hundred miles. We are about an hour away. It's different than where I come from. The violence of the storm makes me wish we were closer.

I take in the newness of the landscape, the elevation, the vegetation, the minor differences that distinguish this place from everywhere else. We are at ease now.

When he reaches inside my shorts to touch me, it feels as if he's found what I hide from everyone. The desire and the cynicism. Hope, too. I grab at his hand, either to push it away or keep it there, I'm not sure. The music goes off or is drowned out by the rain. I hear only my own sounds. I don't think I've ever made them before. I feel far away.

When I put my lips to him, he shudders. At either the desire fulfilled or exposed. It is him and me here—now— and it is also as if we've played these roles over and over. Familiar and new each time.

"At least the tension is over now," he says.

We were minutes away.

I rest my hand on his shoulder again. "That's good, right?"

The radio plays. I think of the concert I'm going to next week when this will all have been a dream. But dreams have a way of turning in on themselves, becoming memories, as the day has turned into a memory already. The car will stop. I will get out and stand in my driveway. I will kiss my husband hello and this man—whom I know best and least of all— will leave, and life, or what we call living, will resume.

But we are not there yet so I sing along with the radio. He joins me. His voice is softer than I expect, detached. For a moment the music is in sync with the windshield wipers.

"Are we heading right into it?" I ask.

Thin streaks of lightning peel down the sky to the east. I close my eyes and count, waiting for the thunder, but it doesn't come or I've missed it. There are more cars on the highway now, more houses and barns alongside. Flashing lights announce an upcoming intersection.

"I think we've skirted around it," he says. "The worst is behind us."

When he points, I look at his fingers. They are strong and

rough in a way I've always desired. Commanding. If you're following, you don't have to think. No choices to make. It has been easy with him.

The air is chilly and I pull my shirt back on. The other cars have slowed, big rigs are passing us and they can see me. He watches me cover up again, relieved, I think, but doesn't say anything. It rains again.

He was wrong. The worst is above us right now. We slow to a crawl, the red taillights of the car in front of us a beacon.

"I'll watch you," he says. "That's okay, right?"

"It's the middle of the day."

"I won't even watch then. I just want to hear you. You seem so far away."

Suddenly I'm conscious of the shorts I'm wearing, the shirt I've taken off again, the bra that does not cover me completely. I didn't brush my hair, put on mascara or even wash my face this morning. We were in a hurry. But he wants me. He wants me like this, even though I'd given up the idea that things could continue, that anything would exist once we got out of the car. I want to hold his desire, let it grow until something unavoidable happens. We have so much further to go.

"Maybe." I shift in my seat.

"It's behind us, I think," he says.

I turn to watch the darkness grow in the rear window. Somehow I missed the transition between the storm and the clear sky that stretches before us. The freeway is dry and wind has blown the last drops of water from the windows.

"You've been wrong before," I say and close my eyes.

We are silent for miles. The music continues. It rains but not as hard as before. The landscape changes from dairy farms with red barns to brown desert with nothing to look at. It's just for a little while, he informs me. He's driven this road many times.

"Locals call it Little Sahara," he says. "No matter how much it rains, these six miles remain barren."

In a moment we are back to lush green hills and I close

my eyes. I think of the four weeks we've known each other, how they stand in relief against the rest of my life.

"It's like a goodbye." I believe the words as I say them.

"Yes, a closure."

He is rejuvenated. He turns up the radio and I feel the car speed up. We are nearing the end.

There is no more tension. No more stretch of highway looming before us. We pass through real towns with stoplights, fast food and motels. I want to jump out of the moving car and say to the first person I find, "Can you believe this happened?"

We don't take turns driving, although I offer halfway through.

"You sleep," he says. "I don't mind."

I close my eyes behind my sunglasses, against the glare that beats down. I feel my arm and shoulder beginning to burn. I can't sleep. My heart beats, my body pulses, because of what we want to, but can't, do.

"Too much for you?" he asks.

He turns down the radio and tells me a story about getting lost on an Indian reservation but refusing to stop or let his wife drive. All I hear is the word "wife" pounding into me like the rain that has begun again. I think of the word "husband," how unconnected it is to the man that waits for me at the end of this road. I could not tell him about this trip or the last four weeks. He would not understand and, outside this car, neither would I. Like a dream when you try to explain it.

Though my eyes are closed I try to guess how big the raindrops are against the windshield. He is silent. I can hear his breathing, slow and spacious.

I have to peek.

He points to the name of the company stenciled on the back of the truck in front of us, Climax Mfg. Co. We laugh but he is irritated, too.

"Every time there's room to pass, it's a curve," he says. "Every straightaway has a car."

I don't answer him. I don't think he's waiting for me to. He's in driver mode, weaving up close, then backing off. I could be anyone. I could be no one. I try to pay for gas.

"I'd have to drive this way anyway," he says, getting out of the car.

He doesn't mean to sound callous. I know this. We both have to go this way. We made a deal. He got bored driving alone. I would save airfare. That's what we said. If we stick to that, I think, we will be okay. If we stay in the car and keep our eyes on the road. But we long to veer off because that's what feels like living, at least for the moment. When we get home, logic will seep back and we will be reined in.

As he pumps the gas, I look across the highway, where ponies play in the sudden sunshine next to a red barn. They move slowly, unlike lightning, so I am able to take their photo from inside the car.

I take a photo of him as he come towards me from the cashier's booth. I will want to look at the print later to see if I can detect anything. If his face betrays what he feels about what has, or could have, happened.

"As long as we stay inside the car, we're safe," he says.

It is hailing so hard we can't see the car in front of us, only the blinking yellow of its hazard lights. We are almost there. Another mile and the storm will be behind us. I recognize the landscape and think of my home and the bedroom and the king-size bed in the middle of it. The bed so big that when I'm alone I can stretch out and still not reach the edges.

Spin Cycle

When the heat subsided, the frogs rained down like a bill come due.

Alone in the Aqua-Mat, Audrey watched the aggressive green downpour, the hand-washables limp in her hands. Voices shouted, brakes squealed, car alarms wailed. Croaking frogs filled the street and wind swept through the open front door. When it was over, silence set in. Audrey exhaled and set her delicates on the chipped countertop.

She glanced over her shoulder at the pajamas and socks tumbling in the dryer. She moved to the open door, shielding her face from dozens of frogs jumping past her into the laundromat. Sounds of the frogs leaping into open washing machines—flesh landing on metal—followed her outside.

On the sidewalk, Audrey nudged the tiny creatures aside with the edge of her sandal. Some were dead, others just sat there breathing. The street was silent except for a woman sobbing and the hum of the overhead cable lines. Audrey saw only a sea of green frogs around her, like a moss blanketing a fallen oak. She lifted her gaze. This sudden moss covered not just the street and sidewalks but the tops of cars and bus shelters and the newspaper boxes chained to light posts.

Audrey bent down to peer at the frogs in the gutter, close enough to smell the stink of brimstone or sulfur or whatever it was that clung to the poor creatures. She sniffed, thinking of high school biology when a boy dared her to lick a frog before they dissected it. He told her that's how people got high. Who, she asked him, could be that desperate?

Her next thought, *Where in the world,* was interrupted by the sight of a frog looking up into her face. No time for this to register as the frog croaked at Audrey and jumped into the air. Another frog croaked, then another, until the entire street was croaking and hopping around like popcorn in hot oil.

Audrey jumped back, landing on a frog, the flesh turning to mush under her heel. She looked through the Aqua-Mat window and saw that the dryer had finished, her warm clothes waiting for her return.

She stood still as the frogs hopped around her.

Instinct told them to jump but not where to go.

The Good Middle Hours

Late in the afternoon, Mitch Hacomb, peeled down to his undershirt, slacks and bare feet, stared out his living room window. His eyes fixed on the single cloud nosing its way across the dull blue sky. *The storm of the century* is what the newscasters were calling it. The storm of the century—two days of high winds, heavy snow, sleet and hail—was coming that weekend and Mitch's house was in its path. It was only the fourth goddamn year of the century, Mitch had complained to his wife, Catherine. How did they know this was the one?

Mitch wiped sweat from his forehead, his gaze drifting down to earth. Across the street, Robert Finnegan, the tall attorney with two ex-wives, scurried around his lawn as if the storm was bearing down that very moment. Mitch sensed similar activity at the other houses on the hill. One last mow, a final swipe at the gutters, a grasp of errant leaves before they were buried in snow. Mitch glanced north across the valley to the hills on the other side. Nothing but clear sky. Mitch nodded to himself. He, for one, wasn't going to be fooled.

Long ago in college, Mitch worked as a copy boy for the local television station. When he had a break between fetching and cleaning, he watched Keith "Apples" Apelbaum crank the radar machine. It was just a television hooked up to a satellite receiver, but in those days, long before Doppler and all that nonsense, it was like a trip to Mars.

One day, after a nasty storm dumped two feet of snow, the machine broke. Apples shrugged his shoulders and looked at the sky through the window, then left to film his segment. The rest of the winter, Apples' method proved to be no more accurate, or inaccurate, than the machine's, and so Mitch turned his back on weathermen, satellites, radar and, when it came along, the Weather Channel. Every morning since that day, Mitch simply stood at the window in his dress socks and briefs, and looked at the sky for his weather report.

Looking south, the view was partially obstructed by Annie's house next door. He could only see part of the southern skies. But it didn't matter; he knew they were clear as well. Since the New Year, they had two weeks of clear weather, followed by two days of snow, then some rain. Now, another two weeks without snow and the weather was dipping down below ten degrees. Too cold to snow. Mitch knew he had another week before he needed to repair the roof at the back of the house.

Across the street, Richard scooped the final leaves into a bag. Seeing Mitch in the window, he waved. Mitch raised his hand in response.

"You could do that, too, you know," Catherine said behind him. "Storm's coming."

Mitch turned from the window but only caught a glimpse of Catherine's skirt disappearing into the kitchen.

"Do you always have to set the thermostat to eighty degrees?" he called after her. "How about sixty-eight for once?"

When she didn't answer, Mitch turned back to the window, crossing his arms and digging his thumbs into his damp armpits. Some people found comfort in the rituals of winter—changing of the seasons, battening down the hatches, that sort of thing. Mitch was sure Catherine and both their children, Robin, a college freshman in Florida, and Nicky, a seventeen-year-old who hardly noticed anything, would say that about Mitch. But Mitch was tired of doing the same things. Not tired in the sense that he wanted to do something else — he was too old for initiative — but he wanted something else to happen.

A moment later, Annie's black SUV pulled into the driveway. She stepped out of the car, set her bag on the porch, and began to drag her empty trashcans from the curb to the garage.

Mitch couldn't remember exactly when Annie moved into the two-story Cape Cod. One day she was just there with her SUV too big for her slight, boyish body and halo of brownish-gold hair.

All Mitch knew was that Annie was a schoolteacher and that she lived alone with a border collie who never barked. They never spoke more than the usual neighborly greetings. Maybe she was divorced, maybe never married; Mitch couldn't tell the difference any more. He also knew, from watching out the window, that she was pulling in and out of the driveway with a different gentleman every few weeks. When Mitch complained about this to Catherine, she said it wasn't true.

"Some of them last a couple months," she would say. "Nice to have choices, you ask me. Besides, is it your business?"

He could have said that Annie reminded him of Robin, that he was afraid that it meant Robin was also casual with men. But really, he just didn't think it was right for people to be so frivolous. He had found a mate and settled down like he was supposed to. Why shouldn't everyone else?

Annie opened the back of the SUV and reached up to grab something dark and bulky. A second later, Mitch realized she was attempting to unload a snow blower by herself. He pulled on his shirt and shoes and hurried through the kitchen, ignoring Catherine's questions.

"Need some help with that?" Mitch called as he approached her on the driveway.

Annie nodded at him, relieved.

Mitch grabbed the wheels. "You get inside and lift it down by the handles."

"Won't be too heavy for you?" Annie ducked her head as she scrambled around the machine.

Mitch shrugged. As they lifted it down, Mitch tried not to grimace as his back knotted up. After they set it down, he stretched his arms overhead.

"I hate to tell you," he said. "You won't need this. Even if it snows, won't be much."

"Weatherman said it'll be the worst of the season." Annie ran her fingers through her hair, making the curls stand up even higher.

"Just hope you got a good deal."

"Did okay, I think." Annie grinned her lopsided smile. "Tougher than I look."

Her smile ate right through him. No wonder she had so many men, Mitch thought. He looked up and down her small body. A flash surged through him. She was older than his daughter, so it wasn't protectiveness. It was possessiveness. He nodded his head to jar loose the feeling. "Need help getting it to the garage?" he stammered out.

"Think I can wheel it in."

"If you need anything." Mitch gestured to his house. "Be happy to lend you Nicky."

"He looks like a nice, strong boy."

"Seriously, you just knock right there." He pointed to the side door.

Annie squinted at him and nodded. Mitch went back to the house trying to think of anything but Annie and her men. In the kitchen, he accepted a pickle from Catherine and resumed his place at the window until dinner was ready.

After dinner, Mitch returned to the living room to sit in his chair with the crossword puzzle. Nicky had bolted right after dinner, running outside to God knew where, to do God knew what. Since Nicky had reached seventeen without getting arrested or seriously injured, Mitch figured his job as a father was done and quit keeping tabs on him.

As he worked the puzzle, Mitch heard Catherine washing the dishes. She would be finished in ten minutes, then come in and pick up her knitting. They had a television in the living room, but only Nicky watched it there. Mitch and Catherine watched television, rather than have sex, in their bedroom. He rested the puzzle in his lap for a moment, listening to Catherine in the kitchen.

He wanted to suggest to Catherine that they take advantage of Nicky being out for the night. Something about Annie and the unique knowledge that he was right about the storm had revived him.

As he debated how to phrase it, Catherine came into the room. Her heart-shaped face was flushed and her hair was coming loose from its clip. She glanced at Mitch as he looked her up and down, noting the ample differences between her and Annie.

"I'd like to make love to you, Cat," Mitch said simply.

Catherine reached up to refasten her hair clip. "Feeling fat today," she replied, picking up her knitting. She settled into the couch and soon the familiar sound of metal against metal bore into Mitch.

Deflated, he lifted the puzzle again. There was no room for negotiation. Catherine steadfastly refused to have sex unless she was feeling thin. She also refused unless she had just taken a shower, brushed her teeth, had fresh sheets on the bed and wasn't thinking about what to cook for dinner or how much laundry was in the hamper. Mitch knew it all by heart. And she *was* fat. There was no other word for it. That didn't mean he didn't want to have sex with her. She was fat and he was bald. Those were the facts. But they so rarely had sex that he wanted to scream, "I don't care if you're fat, dirty, hairy, smelly…I just want to have sex!"

But of course he didn't scream at Catherine. He never did. Her exactitude was bigger than both of them. He would simply keep at her for a few weeks. Eventually, she would give in. Mitch had never strayed and never would. Catherine knew it, too, ninety percent of the time. Her giving in that final ten percent ensured it.

Mitch liked to think that they were reckless when they were first married but that wasn't true. She had always been exact and he loved her for it, just as she indulged his insatiable appetite those first few years.

After ten minutes, Catherine set her knitting down and went into the bathroom in the hallway. Mitch waited one second, two, then heard the tiny click of the lock on the bathroom door. He threw the puzzle across the room where it smacked the darkened television screen and dropped to the carpet. That tiny click. All because one day on their honeymoon, a hundred years earlier, he burst in on her, hoping for spontaneous sex, just as she was stepping naked into the shower. She had been mortified and screamed at him until he backed out of the room in shame, his erection lost for days.

When the bathroom door opened, Mitch heard Catherine go upstairs and, a moment later, the low hum of the television from their bedroom. He retrieved the crossword puzzle and smoothed the paper with the heel of his hand. He settled back into the chair and chewed on the pencil, trying to recapture the calm mood of the day. Normally, that was his favorite time of the day—after dinner, before bedtime.

When they were first married, those were the hours he and Catherine collapsed into bed together, talking and laughing and making love. When the kids came along, Catherine gave them baths at that time. They lived in a smaller house then. Mitch would sit in the living room reading the newspaper and listening to their giggles from down the hall.

For a few years, he smoked a pipe. Robin loved the smell and would hang onto his armchair in her nightgown and wet hair, watching him pack tobacco into the bulb. If Catherine wasn't around, Mitch let Robin hold the pipe to her mouth for a moment. Then he took it into his own mouth and sucked in while lighting the pungent leaves. Robin would flare her tiny nostrils, trying to catch the scent.

Even now, when he sat alone in the living room, he found some measure of peace in those hours. Not exactly happiness, Mitch admitted, but it was close.

He wanted to call Robin, though he had no idea what to say. Robin was a no-nonsense girl, just like her mother. She wouldn't understand her father calling just because he missed her. Mitch smoothed the puzzle on his lap again. Robin was due to call on Sunday. He could wait.

Saturday, after a lunch of tuna sandwiches and pickles, Nicky disappeared to his room while Mitch helped Catherine carry the dishes to the sink.

"Seriously," she began. "It worries me."

"It doesn't worry me." Mitch ran water over a sand-colored plate, wondering how many times it had been washed during the years. "We'll have another week of mild weather and I'll start next weekend. Besides, I don't have all the supplies."

"Could borrow some from Robert. He has everything."

Mitch shook the water from his hands and looked at Catherine. She was trying to appeal to his sense of competition but she didn't even know where to find that part of him. Mitch made a cutting motion across his neck and left the kitchen, wiping his hands on his pants.

From the living room, he could hear the music from Nicky's room. Mitch huffed up the stairs and banged Nicky's door open.

"Can't you play any other album?" Mitch searched the stereo for the power button.

Nicky was kneeling on his bed, looking out the window. At the sound of Mitch's voice, he jumped off the bed, catching a finger in the blinds.

"Album?" Nicky snorted. "They're called CDs now, Dad."

"I know what they're called," Mitch snapped. "What's going on?"

"Nothing." Nicky clicked off the stereo. "I'll put on the headphones."

Mitch reached over the bed and pulled the cord so hard that it broke, leaving the blinds lopsided. Out the window, he quickly saw what held Nicky's attention. The window looked across to Annie's house and into her bedroom. There she was, twenty feet away, naked and on top of one of her men.

It was like watching live television. The man's face was

out of view, but Annie—her face, body, hair, everything—was perfectly framed by the window, nothing but two panes of glass between her and Mitch.

Mitch looked at Annie's breasts and her backside. Her eyes were closed, her body relaxed, her jaw slack—like she was performing a routine she knew by heart. But she wasn't smiling. Of all that he was seeing, that was most shocking.

"You watch this often?" Mitch didn't take his eyes from Annie's face.

"She should close her blinds," Nicky answered.

"You shouldn't watch."

"Jesus, Dad, I've seen more on cable." Nicky walked out of the room. Mitch knew he was heading for another root beer, the sight of Annie's breasts already pushed aside by the thought of a cold drink.

Mitch looked out the window again. Annie was now prostrate over the man. Her head was turned toward the window, but she had tucked her face into the crook of the man's arm.

"Mitch!" Catherine called up the stairs. "Contractor's on the phone."

He jerked the broken string and the blinds cascaded down. "I told you I wasn't worried," he yelled back.

After dinner, Catherine went to the bedroom to nurse a migraine. Nicky had been picked up by some friends. Mitch paced around the house, too unsettled to work the crossword.

Ten minutes later, Mitch stood at the window inside Nicky's room, listening to the silence from his own bedroom. Catherine didn't sleep or watch television during a migraine, just laid in the dark with a compress over her eyes. If they were lucky, the migraine would be gone by morning.

Mitch left the blinds down, parting the slats carefully with his fingertips. He watched Annie's dark window for a few minutes before noticing two figures in the bed, under the covers. Their feet rested on pillows, their heads at the foot of the bed. Soon they began to move.

Mitch's throat ached with jealousy as Annie climbed on

top of the man. He watched them for a few minutes, his fingers in the blinds. He had seen his share of stag films but nothing like this: real people having real sex. It didn't feel pornographic, just incredibly intimate. Like reading a woman's diary.

A few minutes later, the man sat up and then, in one motion, lifted Annie up and tucked her underneath him. Mitch could see a tattoo on the man's left shoulder and his massive legs and backside. All he could see of Annie was the outline of her hair pressed into the bed. Mitch couldn't imagine she liked being trapped like that. He let go of the blinds and stood motionless in the dark.

Faint light filtered through the blinds. He wanted to turn away. He saw himself walk down the stairs, back to his chair and puzzle. He would snap on the lamp and finish all but a few words, refusing to use a crossword dictionary. Then he'd climb the stairs again and lay in the bed next to Catherine, who, if she wasn't asleep, would pretend to be.

Mitch slid a finger between two slats again. A light was on in Annie's bathroom. The small, high window was frosted so Mitch could only see a shape moving behind it. He imagined Annie's naked shoulders and neck. She moved toward the window and he imagined her breasts and arms as she reached for something on the windowsill: a toothbrush, a cotton ball. Suddenly another shape appeared behind her and the two figures merged into one. The light snapped off and they were all plunged into darkness again.

"Mitch! Phone!"

At Catherine's scream, meant for him downstairs working on his puzzle, Mitch jumped from the window, his slight erection fading as his heart raced.

"In here," he called out, looking around Nicky's room.

Catherine pushed open the door with one hand, holding the cordless phone in the other. A wet washcloth was draped on top of her head, the corners hanging into her face.

"Didn't you hear the phone ring?" she asked.

Mitch shook his head, gesturing to the clothes strewn across the floor. "Always amazes me what a slob he is."

Catherine looked doubtfully at Mitch. "Here." She held
out the phone. "Talk to your daughter. Seems to think she's
not coming home for Christmas."

"It's Saturday," Mitch said.

Catherine shrugged and left the room.

"I'm staying in Florida, Daddy," Robin said from the other
end of the phone. "I can't take any more snowy winters. I'm
in love with the beach."

Mitch turned his back to the window so he wouldn't be
tempted to look. He pressed the phone to his ear, trying to
concentrate on his daughter's voice.

"Won't be much snow this winter," he said.

"I'm serious, Daddy. Going to feed the homeless."

"What, when it dips below sixty-five?"

"You're such a cynic."

"You'll break your mother's heart," he said.

"Can't worry about that," she answered. "Anyway, I
wanted to tell you. I solved the problem with the church."

"Which problem is that?" Mitch asked. "The woman-
priest problem or the gay-marriage problem?"

"My problem." She sighed. "Haven't had time on
Sundays. Interferes with the gym."

"Interferes?"

"Can't do both. But, anyway, I found this channel on cable
where they televise Mass on Sundays. So I can follow the
service while on the Stairmaster at the gym. Even bring my
own box of grape juice and a piece of bread for Communion."

"And you do all this while you are on...the what...the
Stairmaster?"

"It's closed-captioned, since the gym is so noisy. Especially
on Sundays." She laughed but Mitch didn't catch why.
"Sometimes, they have another priest who does sign
language while he performs Communion."

"Do you know sign language?" Mitch was confused. What
was his daughter learning at that college? What did sign
language have to do with criminology, which was what she
was supposed to be studying? Moreover, what did it have to
do with Communion?

"Can't you just go to church like normal people?" he asked.

"I'm a busy person, Daddy." Her voice was business-like, betrayed only by the little girl endearment she'd never given up. "In fact, I have a study group now and a meeting for a lecture we're sponsoring on 'Roles for Women in Police Dramas.' Sorry about Christmas. Can't be helped. Tell Mom." She made a kissing sound. "Love you."

Later that night, as he listened to Catherine's sounds behind the locked bathroom door, Mitch thought about Robin on the Stairmaster, staring up at a black and white image of a priest on television. It wasn't the television that was hard to comprehend, it was his daughter. His little Rockin' Robin making her own decisions. More determined already in her life than he had ever been in his.

Early the next morning, Mitch was bundled in a red wool cap, gloves and hiking boots, surveying the perimeter of the house. The sky was overcast. He chewed on a piece of toast as he studied the double-paned windows he installed the summer before.

Mitch paused at the garage to check the thermometer. Nine degrees. That kind of temperature separated the boys from the men. Mitch looked at his neighbors' backyards. Nobody was outside except him and a couple squirrels scrapping for food near the shed. He threw the crust at them.

In the low forties, there were always a few diehards, like their mailman, wearing shorts around town. In the thirties, it usually snowed and the enthusiasts were ready to trade cold for snow sports. At twenty degrees, everyone stayed indoors to wait it out. But ten degrees and below: that was real weather.

Around the back, Mitch looked up at the collapsed roof. It was over the entrance to the basement so it didn't affect any other part of the house, except for a few gaps where snow and rain came in. Mitch had taped a shower curtain into place, but Catherine wasn't keen on that. It was an eighty-year-old house, Mitch had explained to her.

"What do you expect me to do?" he asked.

"To keep it up," she answered.

Sensible enough, he thought, but he knew he had time. He walked around the corner so he was between his house and Annie's. He looked up at her bedroom window, surprised to see the blinds drawn. He glanced at the frosted bathroom window but in the muted daylight it was hard to tell if the light was on.

A window opened above Mitch. Catherine leaned her head out the bedroom window.

"TV says the storm will be here by noon." She frowned at him. "You have about four hours."

Mitch shook his head. He would like to get her up on the roof, just once. She'd see what he was up against.

"Four hours isn't enough," he called up.

"So don't prepare for the whole winter," she shouted. "Just this one storm."

Mitch backtracked around the house, refusing to look at the roof. He glanced again at the thermometer. He grabbed it between his gloved hands. It read twelve degrees. Three degrees in less than thirty minutes. If that kept up, it would be warm enough to snow by the afternoon.

Inside the house, Mitch didn't bother taking off his boots as he climbed upstairs to Nicky's room. Nicky was gone. Always gone, Mitch thought. He'd be at college next year, leaving Mitch and Catherine alone with their empty, eighty-year-old, broken-down house.

He pulled open the blinds using what was left of the broken string. Annie's blinds were still drawn but that wasn't what held his attention. Beyond her house, he saw the enormous, thick-bottomed clouds coming towards him, their shadows long and deep across the valley. He watched the sky, wondering to himself if something had happened and he missed it.

The clouds moved faster. It was going to be bad. Not bad enough to talk about until the end of the century, but bad enough that Catherine would forever remind him of this weekend.

Annie's SUV pulled in. She was alone, dressed in a heavy

jacket and baseball cap. Brow furrowed, she unloaded a big bag of salt, struggling to carry it up her front steps.

Mitch considered helping her. He thought of her breasts behind the opaque bathroom window. Then he thought of Robin at her gym in lukewarm Florida, taking Communion while she sweated out her youth. Suddenly, Catherine was behind him, next to Nicky's bed, close enough that he could smell her shampoo.

A Divorced Man's Guide
to the First Year

First, you will move into a dismal apartment on the other side of town.

It will have one bedroom. You will consider two-bedroom places but your sixteen-year-old daughter informs you she will never sleep anywhere but her own bed and when you calculate rent plus mortgage on your ex-house, you realize the extra room isn't worth it.

You will call it the Man Cave. This last trace of romanticism in you tries to make the shithole apartment sound better than the stains on the walls, the third-hand carpet and the bathroom that grosses out even you.

You will realize that, in addition to many other things, your wife made you appreciate a clean bathtub and toilet.

You will spend an inordinate amount of time cleaning the Man Cave though you will never invite anyone, except your eleven-year-old son, inside.

You won't have a television. You will watch the big game at your buddy's house, in his well-appointed den, drinking his beer and watching his giant flat screen TV that is exactly like the one in your ex-house. His wife will greet you and offer you food but it is clear from her manner that you are now a bastard.

You will wear the bastard label proudly for a while, until even your son begs off staying at the Man Cave. It smells sad, he tells you. This breaks what is left of your heart. His still-little-boy-smell as you slept next to him was the closest thing to joy you had left in your life.

You will teach your daughter how to drive even though she hates you. She will roll her eyes when you tell her she is a good driver. She thinks you are bullshitting her. That you believe this makes up for being a bastard. But she IS a good driver. This will make you unreasonably proud.

You will spend too much time on Facebook. You resist being 'that guy' until the night that a third beer gives you a why-the-hell-not feeling. You send friend requests to every girl you remember from high school—attractive or not.

You will receive three responses right away. These will be from the ones who are married and fat. The ones you are most curious about will ignore you. You will cyber spy on them for a few weeks.

Nothing will feel as good as you remember: masturbating, reading without interruption, hogging the covers.

You will start to remember only the good things about your wife. You fear she is remembering only the bad about you.

You will be broke all the time.

You will shrug when people ask what happened, then trot out the tired explanations: we were married too young, we grew apart, we weren't in love anymore. You can't remember what actually happened.

One night you will ask your ex-wife and she will loudly, painfully, remind you what actually happened.

You will have one dark night—at least one—when the brutality of the situation can no longer be blunted by alcohol, work, sex or sleep. You have failed. You no longer get to ask her "how was your day?" Whatever was happy and pure in the framed wedding photo you have on the bookshelf no longer exists outside of that moment. You will put the frame into a drawer.

You will miss your dog and must refrain from stealing him when you pick up the kids one Saturday.

You will buy an animal—a rebound pet like a fish or

hamster—that you will forget to care for. Your daughter will find its lifeless carcass and it will take you two weeks to realize her white hot anger is not about a dead animal.

You will start lifting weights.

You will attend to a rock concert with a woman in her twenties and your ears will ring for days.

You will humiliate yourself putting on a condom.

A never-married female co-worker will offer to take you shopping for new clothes. You want to find her attractive but you just don't.

You will buy some house plants and diligently water them.

You will no longer notice the looks of pity on your co-workers' faces.

You will no longer deny that the rebound girl was a rebound.

You will move into a bigger, cleaner apartment. You ask your wife, in a moment of civility, if she will help decorate it.

You will go to dinner at your ex-house and you will enjoy it. Your children will no longer beg for you to move back home.

You will begin to see beyond your own misery.

Finally, slowly, the fissures in your heart will begin to scar over.

SHAKESPEARE'S GARDEN

Sunday evening in the garden, as she reaches farther into the rosebush, Evelyn feels a twinge in her left knee. Shifting her weight on the gardening pad doesn't make a difference. Evelyn sighs, stands up and tucks the clippers into her cardigan pocket. She is done for now. Shakespeare, presiding over the patch of heather in the corner, says to her, "Go."

Evelyn has been waiting for this sign. The chimes on the back porch chorus in the dusk. The moon casts a soft light across the roses standing tall under Shakespeare's gaze. Evelyn listens but the sound of his voice has faded and she is alone again. She rubs one hand with the other and looks at the pile of pruned branches. There is so much to do if she is going to go.

With aching knees, Evelyn walks along the stone pathway. Shakespeare's eyes and unsmiling lips have not moved but the word echoes around her. She rests her hand on his cold head, the band of her wedding ring clinking against the concrete. His head is damp, as if water is seeping from the inside. By this she knows it will rain tomorrow, even though tonight every star in the sky is visible. Evelyn looks forward to the clouds and rain. It will feel, for a few days at least, like the garden she visits in her dreams.

With the sleeve of her sweater, Evelyn rubs the moisture

101

off the base of Shakespeare's bust. When she is sure he has
no more words for her, Evelyn walks inside to the kitchen. A
stack of bills sit on the countertop. Dirty dishes wait in the
sink and Richard has thrown the bed sheets on top of the
washing machine. It is no one's fault, she thinks, rubbing her
face. The sounds of the Trailblazers' game drift from the living
room. As Richard dozes on the couch, the cat curled next to
him, Evelyn calls Maggie.

"What did Richard say?" Maggie asks.

"Just book the ticket, please," Evelyn whispers. "I can't
wait any longer."

Next, Evelyn calls Janey, her daughter, who worries about
Richard being alone. That's why she is calling, Evelyn
explains. They are on the phone only a few minutes. Evelyn
can hear the cadence of Richard's breath, his hiccup when
the volume on the television grows louder during the
commercials. In thirty-eight years, they've never been apart
for more than a day.

Janey was six when they moved into the house. Evelyn
claimed the kitchen and backyard as her own and Richard
set himself up on the front porch.

"A real how-do-you-do kind of porch," he liked to say.

Richard set up two wicker chairs, a small table and a
transistor radio. He sat there in the evenings listening to
baseball games and playing chess with Janey. On Sunday
afternoons, he worked the crossword puzzle and talked to
their neighbor, Mr. Keegan. Evelyn never liked the front
porch; she felt too exposed.

She preferred the shelter of the backyard, though her first
attempts at a vegetable garden yielded a meager bounty.
Janey drifted between them—bringing a tomato or squash
to Evelyn then playing chess with Richard until bedtime.

One day, when Janey was twelve, she saw a poster about
Portland's Shakespeare Garden and begged to go. In the
middle of an April rainstorm, Evelyn and Janey found
Shakespeare's alcove tucked behind a row of cypress trees in
the Rose Garden. Evelyn stood under an umbrella while

Janey wandered through the budding bushes writing their names in a notebook.

Each rose bush and flower had a sign bearing the plant name and its origin. Prospero from *The Tempest* was a tall, spiky bush that in the summer would offer enormous red roses. Fair Bianca from *The Taming of the Shrew* was a small bush showing just a wisp of the white paper-thin roses to come. A few names sounded familiar to Evelyn—Ophelia, Tatiana—but she couldn't place them. She hadn't read much Shakespeare. Strawberry plants bearing tiny fruit were nestled in the ground between the roses. Janey ate one before Evelyn could stop her. Etched into the sidewalk below a statue of William Shakespeare was the phrase, *Of all flowers, methinks a rose is best.*

"I don't want just roses," Janey declared.

For days, Janey looked for references to flowers and herbs in a library edition of *Shakespeare's Complete Plays and Sonnets* while Evelyn dug through a weathered copy of *Hooper's Guide to Gardening* to learn what woodbine (honeysuckle), oxlips (primrose) and dewberries (blackberries) were. Next Evelyn sketched a diagram of grass, flowerbeds, bench, statue and vegetable garden.

With guidance from the local nursery, she and Richard built flowerbeds around the perimeter of the yard. The new vegetable garden, wrapping around the edge of the garage, would be twice as big as the original. Next came a three-tiered bed that sloped down the southern wall. At the top, they planted honeysuckle and jasmine. In the middle, primrose. At the bottom would be the herb garden. The back wall didn't need much work. The cypress trees behind the fence, like the ones in the Portland garden, were a natural backdrop to the full-grown rose bushes they planted—vintage, antique, crossbreeds and thoroughbreds. Janey drew handmade signs for each bush, which were replaced six months later by embossed metal ones that Evelyn had ordered.

In the fall, Evelyn and Janey buried bulbs deep in the soil next to the back porch steps and planted purplish-pink and yellow-blue pansies ('love-in-idleness,' Shakespeare called them) as groundcover. In the spring, the tulips and daffodils would burst into a ribbon of color.

A year after they began, they installed the final touch: Shakespeare's corner. Richard cleared the ground and lifted the bust onto the concrete stand he had poured. Around Shakespeare, the heather bloomed into a base of brilliant pink flowers from July to September. Next to him, they placed a wooden bench with iron scrollwork.

At first, Evelyn sat on the bench only to rest while Janey watered the roses or weeded the vegetables. When the days grew longer, Evelyn sat on the bench after dinner and tried to read Shakespeare's plays. It was so laborious, one finger on the line of text, another on the footnotes, that Evelyn could only read a few pages each night. Gradually, though, the words began to fall into her and reading was no longer a struggle. Evelyn found herself retreating to the garden at odd times of the day and night. When no one was watching, Evelyn would rest her hand on Shakespeare's head, feeling a connection to him, as if he were trying to tell her something. It wasn't until later that she associated the temperature of his head with the coming weather.

The garden brought Janey closer to Evelyn than she'd ever been. They spent hours in the garden on weekends, planting and pruning, cleaning up or planning for the next season. But when Janey began her junior year in high school, she abandoned the garden. After college, she roamed through Europe and Asia, coming home only long enough to save up for her next trip. Now in her late thirties, Janey was living in Paris. Occasionally, Evelyn sent her seed packets.

"How's your garden?" Evelyn asked now and then.

"It's coming along," was all Janey would ever say.

The morning after Shakespeare spoke, rain drips off the broken gutter and wakes Evelyn from a hazy sleep. She should have replaced the gutter when she felt Shakespeare's head but she hates those kind of chores. There is also a broken doorknob to fix and two light bulbs to replace. Those had been Richard's responsibilities.

At seven, the clock chimes in the living room and Richard begins to stir. His hot body is too close; Evelyn throws the covers off her legs. Using his right arm, he lifts his left leg, shifts closer to Evelyn and rests again.

The stroke happened more than a year ago, just after Richard retired. They were in the kitchen on a Sunday morning when he dropped the cereal bowl he was carrying. Evelyn reached for a dishtowel without looking up from the newspaper until Richard groaned, crumpling into her as she rose from the table.

Of those first six months, Evelyn remembers only the phone ringing and the roses looking restless. She went into the garden just once a day, too nervous to leave Richard's side for very long. His speech gradually improved and Evelyn helped him learn to dress, eat and speak again, almost—but not quite—like he used to. His face had changed, too. The left side drooped slightly lower than the right; the corner of his mouth permanently tugged into a faint grimace. The stroke itself hadn't hurt, he told Evelyn once. Only living with it was painful.

Through it all, Evelyn woke up each morning and looked out the bedroom window at the garden below. Despite her meager care, it did not wither. But Richard grew tired of struggling up the stairs, so they moved from the bedroom with its handmade bed and view of the garden into the room behind the kitchen, which looked onto the street. They crammed into a narrower bed, touching hip to toe all night long. Evelyn had not slept well since.

She planted a window box of chervil and mint to block the view but it wasn't the same. Some nights, when she was sure Richard was sleeping, she slipped out of bed to walk through the garden.

Janey came home only once since Richard's stroke, a languid weekend where she acted as if nothing had happened. During the day, she sat with Richard on the porch playing chess and once took him to a Trailblazers' game. In the evenings, she helped Evelyn trim back the honeysuckle but Evelyn saw that her thoughts were elsewhere. Janey chatted incessantly about life in Paris, hardly paying attention to the shears in her hand or the smell of winter around them. Evelyn waited patiently, breathing in the aroma of pine needles and fireplaces, but in four days Janey never once asked Evelyn how she was doing.

When the clock strikes eight, Evelyn sits up in bed.

"Are you going to go?" Richard whispers next to her.

Evelyn hesitates, surprised that his voice is so clear, almost like before.

"Yes," she says, clearing her throat. "Janey is coming to stay with you. You'll be fine."

"Janey's coming today?"

"No." It all comes out in a rush. "In April, when I go to London. I was able to get the package for the birthday celebration. The royal garden will be in full bloom."

"Oh...you're going to go."

"That's what you asked, isn't it?"

He is quiet for a few seconds and then pulls himself up on one side to look at her. His cheek is creased from the pillowcase. His green eyes search her face. "I meant going to the store...for the gutter," he says. "I didn't know you made up your mind. We were supposed to talk about it." He collapses, breathless, back against the pillows.

"I need to go...I'm going." Evelyn tries to slow her own speech.

"If you just wait a few more months," he says, "maybe I can go with you."

"His birthday's in April." Evelyn speaks softly, edging out of the bed. She wonders if Janey could really be trusted with the roses.

"It's that important to you?" Richard's voice cracks. "You want to go without me?"

"It's only once a year."

"Maybe I'll come. Why not? I'll try..." He hoists himself up and swings his legs over the side of the bed. "I'll fix the gutter."

"Don't be ridiculous, sweetheart. You never wanted to go

before." She touches his shoulder but he shrugs her off. "I'll do it this afternoon," she says. "I promised, right?"

"Remember when you tried to fix the screen door and nailed it shut instead? I'll take care of it. All of it."

"It'll just be a couple weeks. Ten days."

"We'll see. Okay. Just…we'll see."

Evelyn crosses the room to the window and parts the curtain. The car sits in the driveway, its fender dented from an accident two years ago. She hears Richard behind her pulling on his robe with great effort. She is used to his gruff, throaty sounds as he struggles with what used to be a simple task. She doesn't move to help him.

At eleven-thirty, there is a break in the rain. It is already the middle of March, almost too late to plant for spring, so Evelyn must hurry. She needs to finish the roses and plant something in the bottom herb bed. She doesn't want Janey to do anything but water.

In the garden, Evelyn stands before Shakespeare, wondering whether to plant rosemary or thyme. Rosemary, the footnotes tell her, is a symbol of remembrance at weddings and funerals. It would hold up best under the cool weather but is prone to grow wildly, leaving its prickly stalks rough and useless. Thyme is more appealing but delicate and won't last more than a few weeks. Evelyn can't resist feeling rosemary is too serious for spring. Because of Ophelia, Evelyn associates it with winter and endings. She settles on the thyme as Shakespeare says quietly, "Yes." Evelyn turns away from his voice.

In front of the rose bushes, Evelyn loads the pruning into a lawn bag. It takes longer than expected and she doesn't leave for the hardware store until after lunch, having convinced Richard, she thinks, to rest on the couch. Evelyn watches him for a few minutes before she leaves. His eyes are closed and his body moves slightly under the blanket.

On the slick roads, Evelyn drives cautiously, thinking of Shakespeare's voice. It was low and melodious, and now blurs into her own voice as she repeats "yes" to herself while she drives. The man at the hardware store helps her choose a replacement gutter. With all her questions about how to install it, she is gone for more than an hour. Finally she is back in the car and thinking of *A Midsummer's Night's Dream*, which she is reading again. More than once she has fallen asleep thinking of the flowers in the book and the flowers in her garden. How she has brought them to life. Sometimes, just as she is drifting off, Evelyn hears Shakespeare call out her name in a sharp voice, like fingers snapping.

As Evelyn pulls into the driveway, she sees Richard lying on the porch. He is on his back, his arms reaching out as if swimming backstroke. The front door stands open, stopped by one of his flimsy slippers. A ladder hangs halfway off the porch crushing the hydrangeas below. Evelyn screams and runs past the ladder, up the stairs. She kneels next to Richard, pressing her face to his. She tries to feel his breath but knows she is too late.

"I said I would take care of it," she says. She repeats this louder, again and again, until she is screaming. "If you'd just waited," she weeps into his hair.

She collapses on Richard's chest, his red flannel shirt soft on her face. He loves to be warm, she thinks, always in a flannel shirt or sweatpants. She wants to get a blanket, something, but can't leave him. The wind has picked up, blowing the rain sideways against them. A small lake has formed on the walkway where it dips slightly. One of those things Richard had planned to fix.

The car door is still open, the sensor beeping into the gray day. Mr. Keegan is next to her, rocking on his feet. Evelyn gazes at Richard's face. The muscles have gone slack and she is overcome with relief that the two sides of his face are symmetrical again.

When she returns home from the hospital, Evelyn wanders alone through the house. The lunch dishes are washed and put away. The magazines, playing cards and lidless pens are gone from the kitchen counter and a faint smell of ammonia hangs in the air. Richard had done it all. Even the dust clouds on the hallway floor are gone. Clean laundry is folded in a basket on the couch. Evelyn moves the basket to the floor and lies down. Rain drips off the broken gutter, the phone rings and Shakespeare calls to her from the garden. Evelyn pulls a cushion over her ears.

Three weeks after the funeral, Evelyn goes back into the garden, which feels bigger than before. Underfoot, the grass needs to be cut; the dewy blades tickle through her thin sandals. The empty herb bed nags at her (rosemary or thyme?). The heather, bold and incessant, has taken over Shakespeare's corner. Evelyn hesitates, suddenly weary, when she sees the stone bust.

Janey has come and gone. She arrived the day before the funeral and busied herself around the house, rummaging through Richard's desk and bureau drawers. Organizing, sorting, boxing up, filling the house with activity. She hired men to fixed the gutter and smooth out the walkway. More than once, she tried to coax Evelyn into the garden.

"The roses need you," she said.

Evelyn could only sit on the couch with a *Travel and Leisure* open in her lap, listening for Richard.

Maggie came too, bringing a new ticket for London.

"You missed his birthday," she said, "but you should still go. It'll be good for you."

Evelyn relented. Only the garden was holding her back.

Now kneeling in front of the roses as the sun disappears, Evelyn dips a toothbrush into the bucket of soapy water and begins to clean the signs: Pretty Jessica, Wise Portia, Lordly Oberon. She has ignored them for so long they are almost illegible. While cleaning Tragic Juliet, a tall bush with pale yellow roses and thumbnail-sized thorns, Evelyn feels sudden distaste.

It is so much work, every year, the same weeding and planting. There has never been a moment where Evelyn could say, "It is finished." And it will always be this way. She sits back and lets her gaze unfocus across the flowers so that the colors blur together.

When she has finished cleaning the signs, the clouds have

parted to reveal a full moon. Evelyn rests on the bench, kneading the knots from her fingers. She opens her notebook and begins to write instructions. "For whom?" Shakespeare asks but Evelyn ignores him. She charts what grows best where, how often to water and when to prune, surprised at how much she knows from memory. As the cool night creeps up her legs, she puts down the notebook and tries to imagine London—the museums, the gardens, anything—but cannot turn that corner in her mind.

WELCOME, ANYBODY

Jim sat in the dining room, bouncing a quarter across the table. It missed the juice glass, crashing into the pile of change off to the side. The house was quiet except for the sound of the grandfather clock gearing up to strike noon. The next quarter clinked into the pulp-streaked glass. Jim thought about the afternoon's baseball game. Now he was free to go.

As the clock chimed, Jim heard the garage door open. A moment later, Nancy came through the kitchen door, bringing in a combination of perfume and car exhaust. Jim fished out the sticky quarter and pushed it into the pile.

Nancy stood in the doorway. Jim pictured her in the car a moment ago, checking her hair in the mirror and thinking over details of the Reverend's party. She squinted at Jim as if he were somebody else.

"What is it?" she asked.

Jim thought about lying to her—just for a day or two—while he figured things out.

"Jim?"

"They let me go." He motioned for her to sit down, but she crossed her arms. "Company's restructuring. There'd been rumors. But I'll get something else," Jim continued, "before you know it."

Nancy's eyelids flickered. "Why didn't you tell me?"

"Thought it wouldn't happen to me," he said.

"But it did."

Jim kept talking, trying to reassure her. The severance was fair and he was paid out his vacation. They had some savings. Nancy turned pale when he mentioned filing for unemployment.

"You don't seem too upset," she said.

He shrugged. When Morris, his supervisor, made the announcement, Jim was more worried about being left to clean up the mess than being fired. He was almost relieved when Morris called him into the office. Denise Rudnick cried and even Kevin Stannard, who hated the company, had a wild look in his eye. Jim simply packed up his desk and left. Strange how easy it was—how satisfying—to walk out in the middle of things. It wasn't until Jim entered the quiet house that he felt the edges of panic.

"I'll take care of it." Jim pushed the termination packet across the table but Nancy ignored it. "Besides, I can catch Daniel's game today. Surprise him."

He thought of Daniel on the pitcher's mound. The brown dirt and the chalky resin bag; Daniel's face peering in for the sign; and Jim's father, the Reverend, in the bleachers. The Reverend had been to every game this season. Jim wiped his hands on his pants.

"Maybe this is what I need," he said. "Chance to try something new. Maybe this'll be good for me and Daniel."

"There's nothing wrong between you two!" Nancy burst out. She looked around the house and took a deep breath. "Should I cancel the party?" she asked.

"It means so much to you."

"He's your father."

Jim slammed his hand on the table. "No one needs to know about this, okay?"

"He could be helpful, you know." Nancy's voice was thin.

She always defended the Reverend. Sometimes the three of them—Nancy, the Reverend, and Jim's mother, Gertrude—acted as if Nancy was their daughter and Jim had married in. Gertrude hadn't asked Jim to help plan the Reverend's retirement party. One day she called up Nancy and that was that. Jim knew the details only from overhearing his wife on the phone. The clock struck the half hour. He reached for Nancy but she moved to the sliding glass door.

"Nothing to worry about." She placed her hands on the glass and stared out.

"Just act normal," Jim replied. "We'll talk about it tonight."

"This is anything but normal."

Her voice was calm, betrayed only by the hitch in her shoulders. Jim longed to embrace her but even moving in his chair made her shake her head. She would come to terms with it in her own way. They'd been married long enough for him to know that.

"Just do what you normally would today, sweetie," he said. "Why did you come home, anyway?"

"I picked up the invitations." She peered up at the sky. "Whether you agree with him or not, you have to admire his dedication. He believes what he believes, you know?" She turned back to Jim, the wistfulness gone from her voice as quickly as it had appeared. "Invitations need to go out tomorrow. Will you stuff the envelopes?"

"Didn't the store do all that?"

"Cheaper." Her voice was apologetic. "If you stuff them this afternoon, tonight the three of us can order pizza and address them." She stood still until Jim nodded his head. "And, if you don't mind, maybe you could drop the deposit off at the caterers?"

Back at the table, Nancy handed Jim an envelope from her purse. She let him clasp her hand for a moment before pulling away. Jim followed her into the kitchen, where she took a can of soda from the refrigerator.

"Stay for lunch?"

"I'll take it to go." She grabbed an apple from the fruit bowl.

When she walked by, Jim hugged her but she didn't soften against him. He kissed the top of her hair, wishing he could do something more. How many nights she quieted his mind with her smooth legs, her tender hands that found his before sleep. How many mornings he woke to find her hand still resting in his. Those were always the best days.

"I'm sorry," he said.

"I believe you," she whispered.

Jim stuffed the celery-green invitations into their envelopes for twenty minutes before taking a break. He drank a glass of tap water and wandered from room to room, careful not to disturb the stillness.

Upstairs in Daniel's room, Jim knelt on the twin bed and studied the Xavier schedule taped to the wall. Why shouldn't he go? He was the one practicing with Daniel in the middle of winter, not the Reverend. He taught Daniel to throw the curve. When the season began, Jim tried to schedule meetings around Daniel's games but it hadn't worked out.

The phone rang as he left the room.

"Hello?"

"James?" the voice asked.

"Mother?"

"What's wrong?"

Jim affected a cough. "A little under the weather today. Thought maybe I'd catch Daniel's game."

"Well, which is it?"

"More of the second, I guess."

"Just like your father. He postponed the ladies' guild until tomorrow so he could go."

"Nancy's not here," Jim said.

"I know. I was calling to leave two more names on the answering machine."

She gave Jim the names and addresses. As he was about to hang up, she told him to wait. He heard the Reverend's voice in the background, then his mother came back on the line.

"Will you drive your father to the game?" she asked. "He'd love your company."

Jim smiled despite himself. How she came to believe what she did, he'd never know.

"I'll swing by at two-thirty," he said.

"He says two-fifteen." She laughed. "Afraid it'll sell out."

Jim hung up, thinking of the time that stretched between now and the game, between the job he no longer held and whatever the next one might be.

At the harbor, Jim bought coffee at a kiosk, surprised by the number of people walking around. No one looked in a hurry to go anywhere. *Don't these people have jobs?* he wondered.

The blond at the register smiled as he placed the money in her hand, conscious of the crispness of each bill. They didn't live like kings but he'd done okay. With Nancy's recent promotion, they managed to take an extra trip this year—a long weekend in Ensenada—but they couldn't live on her salary alone.

Jim walked along the boardwalk, gazing at the boats on the bay. Above him, the sun was high into the cloudless sky and a slight breeze had picked up. Ideal baseball weather. Jim caught his reflection in a window, pleased that he had changed from slacks into shorts and his old Xavier hat. Maybe he would grow a mustache. Start jogging again. Rent a boat and spend a week on Mission Bay.

Jim dropped off the check at the caterer's office, forbidding himself to look at the amount. He didn't want to be tempted to interfere just because he had the time. After the caterers, he stopped in front of a cigarette shop and looked at his watch. Still half an hour before he had to pick up the Reverend.

He glanced up at the wooden sign above the shop door. It read *Welcome Anybody* in wood-block letters bordered by a dozen tiny flags painted in primary colors. He stared at the sign for a few minutes, then peered inside the shop. A man leaned against the counter reading a paperback, his thin hands cradling his chin. A horn sounded somewhere behind Jim, prompting him to step into the store.

Before he could think of a reason not to, Jim bought a pack of cigarettes. The man handed Jim the change and looked at him expectantly. Jim wanted to ask him a question— what he was reading, how business was doing, if he owned a boat—but hurried out, feeling the man wanted more than Jim could give.

Outside, Jim stood under the sign and rubbed the package between his fingers. He hadn't smoked in five years. He unwrapped the package, savoring the sound of the cellophane crinkling and the sharp smell of tobacco.

When he put the cigarette between his lips, the earthy feel of the paper was almost enough. Jim imagined his throat tightening, the taste of the smoke, trying to feel as if he'd already smoked it, but the pleasure wasn't there.

Finally, Jim lit the cigarette. It was as good as he remembered—the deep breath, the exhale, the sharp, immediate buzz. He smoked quickly, berating himself to slow down. Fumbling for a second cigarette, he dropped the pack. The women walking by stared at his shaking hands. He lit the cigarette, shoved the pack into his pocket and walked away, coming to rest on a bench on the edge of the harbor.

 He watched a boat nose its way around the jetty to the open sea while the others rocked in the dock. It was unnatural to live in San Diego and not own a boat. He might have forgiven the Reverend for bringing them to California if he had bought a boat, even a kayak. Fortunately, Uncle Frank, Gertrude's brother, visited during the summers that Jim was in high school and rented the same silver motorboat each year.

Uncle Frank took Jim onto the warm waters of Mission Bay three summers in a row. During the day, Jim steered through the water skiers and the hydro-boats from Sea World, practicing his turns and smiling at girls. At night they docked and remained on board long past sunset, eating charred hot dogs and listening to the Padres on a portable radio. Uncle Frank taught Jim how to smoke and how to hide it from the Reverend. For those summers, away from everyone's gaze, Jim pretended Uncle Frank was his father.

Jim drove along the coast, the steering wheel warm in his hands. He loved being on the edge of the world. He could be anybody here, different than at the beach in North Carolina, where, even beyond the breakers in the cold Atlantic water, he couldn't escape being the Reverend's son.

In 1962, the Reverend had been on track to become pastor of St. Andrew's in Asheville, where he served as junior deacon. One rainy January afternoon when Jim returned from school, the Reverend was sitting on the front porch.

"Reverend Harris is not retiring after all, son," he said when Jim climbed the steps and stood before him. "But there's an opportunity for us in California. St. Anne's-by-the-Sea. Just a different ocean."

Jim hated San Diego. The only solace he found was riding his bike to the beach and flinging himself into the sea. The shock of the water, and the knowledge that no one knew where he was, made him invisible. The kids he met on the beach taught him to surf. He began to slip out of church on Sunday mornings, first to surf and later to play baseball. Jim didn't tell his new friends about the Reverend and they didn't ask.

When the Reverend discovered Jim was skipping church, he wasn't angry, which annoyed Jim. Normal fathers yelled at their sons. Instead, the Reverend didn't speak to Jim for nearly a week, then delivered a lecture that lasted three nights. The Reverend spoke relentlessly about the grace of God, the call to service, the meek of the earth and the damned. One night, the Reverend began the story of how he was called to be a minister. Jim had heard it many times and stood up to leave. The Reverend grabbed him by the arm.

"You're smart, son," the Reverend said. "I resisted for so long. I don't want you to go through that."

"I'm not going to be a minister."

"I know that," he said, "but a man without faith is doomed. Like walking a tightrope with no net. Faith is a seatbelt. Don't you understand? God is speaking to you, but you have to listen. You can't listen if you're playing baseball."

"I don't want to listen to God. I want to play baseball." Jim pulled his arm away.

"You can do more than one thing."

"Then why can't you?"

When the Reverend hesitated, Jim left the family room, walking past his mother in the kitchen. Since then, Jim had rarely been inside a church. Even Daniel's baptism in St. Anne's was painful under the Reverend's gaze.

After that, the Reverend gave up on Jim and turned his attention to Daniel. And now, fourteen years later, it seemed to be working. Lately, Daniel was leaving the house early on Sundays for services at St. Anne's. Jim had to hand it to the Reverend. He never gave up.

When Jim turned into his parents' driveway, the Reverend was waiting on the porch. Jim tried to shake off the familiar dread as the Reverend got into the car and buckled up. In his wrinkled black shirt, stiff white collar and Xavier cap, the Reverend looked less imposing than Jim remembered. Jim wanted to ask if he had lost weight but lapsed into his habit of waiting for the Reverend to speak first.

"Wait 'til you see him, James, you won't believe it."

"I see him every day," Jim said. "I coached him during tryouts, remember?"

"This is different." The Reverend waved his hands in the air. "He's so grown up out there. So confident. He doesn't even hear the catcalls from the stands. And he's a natural hitter."

"You only saw three games."

"You should have been there."

"Dad."

"He even drew me a diagram of their pitch strategies. You know, what to throw with a runner on first and one out."

"I played for four years, remember? I know about pitch strategies."

"I don't know if he should really be a pitcher, though. He's got a great swing."

"Of course he's a pitcher." Jim moved the car into the fast lane. If he could manage it, they would only be alone for another ten minutes. "Why would you say that?"

"Anything can happen."

"Yes."

"That's all I'm saying. He needs to keep his options open." The Reverend was silent for a few minutes. "Why aren't you at work?"

"Sick."

When the Reverend didn't answer, Jim glanced at him. He was holding the caterer's receipt Jim had left on the seat.

"Nancy knows what I like," he said. "Shrimp cocktail, calamari."

"What are you talking about?" he asked.

"Daniel's a good boy but he doesn't keep a secret very well."

"Well, don't let on. It's a big deal to Nancy."

"But not to you."

Jim didn't answer. He reached into his shirt pocket, fished out a cigarette and put it to his lips.

"You're not—" the Reverend began.

"I'm not."

They didn't speak the rest of the way. Soon, the road deadended and the green, glorious baseball field lay in front of them.

Jim left the Reverend at the first-base bleachers. They were ten minutes early and Jim was too nervous to entertain the Reverend, so he wandered through the deserted campus.

Jim had been to Xavier many times since his own graduation but now it was Daniel's school. As a starter, Jim had been ten and four, including a win in the first game of the state championships his senior year. But those were ancient memories to anyone Daniel's age, kids who were much bigger and stronger than Jim and his teammates had ever been. Jim had watched Daniel eat his cereal in the morning, back when it was like every other morning. Daniel's legs, too long for the rest of his body, stretched underneath the entire length of the dining room table, kicking Jim every time he moved.

Jim went into the boys' bathroom near the front office and stood in the third stall, searching for the initials he carved into the ceiling years ago. After a few minutes, he located them, amazed they were still there. Jim lit another cigarette, thinking of all the uneasiness he smoked away in high school. Back then he fantasized about playing college baseball and making the majors but no scout ever called.

After graduating, Jim enrolled at junior college. At first he was content to disappear in the anonymity he craved his whole life. No one knew or cared who he was. He didn't realize until he met Nancy that he had grown used to everyone looking past him. She was the first person in years that looked directly into his face and smiled. He often told her that he married her because of that first smile.

Jim called her as he walked back to the bleachers.

"I wanted to hear your voice," he said. "It's about to start."

"Things are going to be okay," she said.

"Things are going to be okay," he repeated.

"Cheer for me, too," she said.

At the top of the bleachers, Jim reached the Reverend just as he stood up. Somewhere below them, a recording of the national anthem began. Jim removed his cap and turned to the field. The grass was a deep, healthy green and an electronic scoreboard, new since Jim's time, was hoisted above the right-field fence.

"He's number eighteen," the Reverend said as they sat down.

"I know." Jim's throat tightened.

When Daniel trotted to the mound, Jim stood and put his hands up to his mouth, preparing to shout. The Reverend pulled him down to the bench.

"Don't," he said. "He doesn't want to know we're here." The Reverend gestured to Xavier's dugout. "The coach, Mr. Martinez, expects Daniel to go far. I talked to him last game. He said if today goes well, Daniel might start against La Jolla."

"Daniel told me."

"Did you know he's batting sixth, not ninth, like most pitchers?"

"What do you think, Dad, I don't know my own son's business?"

The Reverend looked away, his chin lifted. *Good*, Jim thought. They sat in silence for a few minutes, cracking peanuts shells and flicking the red skins off their fingertips.

"Mr. Martinez says his curveball's the best he's seen in a long time," the Reverend said.

"Really?" Jim squinted toward Daniel, trying to discern which pitch he was throwing from that distance. Next time, he'd bring binoculars. "I taught him that curve, you know."

"You didn't throw a curve," the Reverend said.

"Of course I did."

Jim was preparing to lay into the Reverend, but pictured Nancy's face and took a deep breath. He exhaled the anger. The Reverend recited the Xavier players' names to him, their batting order and their stats. Jim was impressed with how much he knew. Maybe instead of attending service, Daniel and the Reverend sat in the sacristy talking ball. He saw them: the Reverend in his white robes and purple bands cloistered with Daniel in the tiny room, heads bent over the playbook as the choir sang in the church. Jim would have gone to church, too, if it had been like that.

He took out a cigarette and rolled it between his fingers. The Reverend raised his gray eyebrows but Jim waved him off. He looked back at Daniel, who pushed and pulled at the brim of his cap. The Vista batter stepped in. Daniel's first pitch sailed far right and rattled against the backstop. He pounded his fist into his glove and picked up the resin bag. His next three pitches were balls and the Vista bench hooted as the batter jogged to first.

"Double 'em up, Saints," Jim called out.

Daniel pitched and the batter hit a grounder to the third baseman who started a double play. Jim saw Daniel's shoulders relax. On the follow-through of the next pitch his rear leg kicked high, like normal. Daniel struck out the next batter on three pitches. The Reverend turned to Jim as Vista took the field.

"So what is it?" he asked. "You're home, you're smoking?"

Jim took off his cap and wiped the sweat from his hairline. The Xavier lead-off hitter stepped up to the plate.

"Well?"

"None of your business."

"Tell me."

"Fine. You want to know?" Jim stood up, his anger bubbling over. "Downsizing, outsourcing, restructuring, expendable middle management, lay-offs, pink-slips, severance package, human resources, exit-interview." Two girls sitting nearby shot Jim looks as his voice grew louder. "How about unemployment insurance, career counseling, update resume, forty-six-year-old unemployed father of today's starting pitcher having to look for a new job. Is that what you want to know?" The girls yelled at Jim to shut up but it felt good to heap it all on the Reverend, who didn't blink or twitch a muscle. Jim slumped back against the warm metal railing.

"And Nancy?" The Reverend's voice was thick with pity. Jim nodded.

"Daniel?"

"Not yet."

The Reverend pulled Jim down to the bench. "If there's anything I can do."

Jim looked at the Reverend but he had turned back to the game, his face indiscernible. The Reverend leaned against Jim, their shoulders just touching. Jim could feel his strength, a rigidity that seemed to work in the Reverend's favor.

"If you kept an eye out for me," Jim said, "that'd be okay."

The Reverend held out the bag of peanuts. Jim dug in.

Xavier maintained their lead through the sixth. In the bottom of the inning, Jim bought sodas from the boosters' table behind the bleachers, then peeked at Daniel in the dugout. He sat in the middle of his teammates with his windbreaker pulled over his right arm, grinning and blowing small bubbles of gum. Jim realized with relief that Daniel was enjoying himself. He was pitching because he wanted to, not because Jim had encouraged him. For a moment, everything felt okay. If only Nancy were there to see it: Jim and the Reverend sitting together, Daniel mowing down the opponents, and the sun shimmering off the outfield grass.

In the seventh inning, Vista tied the score by hitting back-to-back doubles off Daniel. Jim pulled his hat down over his eyes. In the bottom of the inning, with two outs and a runner on second, Daniel got his first hit of the game by beating out an infield grounder. That started a rally that pushed Xavier ahead by four runs. Jim's heart was full as he watched Daniel in the center of it all.

After giving up two runs in the bottom of the eighth, Coach Martinez pulled Daniel and put in a hulking blond-haired boy to protect Xavier's diminishing lead. The boy retired the final batter and then the bottom of the ninth in order, saving the game for Daniel. Jim and the Reverend made their way to Xavier's jubilant dugout.

"You're here," Daniel shouted.

Jim hugged him, feeling the boy's taut muscles through the sweat-soaked jersey.

"Did you see me?"

"You were great, son," Jim said. "First rate. I counted five K's."

"Six." The Reverend slapped his palm against a score sheet. "Here, autograph it for me."

"See, Granddad." He took the sheet. "I needed that extra practice on Sunday."

Jim looked from his son to his father. "You skipped church for baseball?"

"No big deal, Dad. Hey." Daniel became excited again. "I was trying to remember every pitch I threw so I could tell you later. Mike, over there," he pointed at a boy in a leg cast, "is supposed to keep track but he never does. Did you see me beat out that infield ball? They scored it a hit, not an error. I'm three for six." He glanced at Jim, then at the Reverend. "Did you come together?"

Jim avoided the Reverend's eye. "Can you come with us now or do you have to shower here?"

"He showers here," the Reverend said.

"I'll be home soon as I can," Daniel said. "Can't wait to tell Mom."

"We're getting pizza for dinner."

"Double pepperoni, please." Daniel handed Jim a scuffed baseball. "It's the game ball. That's number two."

Daniel left and the dugout emptied. The men walked back to the car in what, Jim realized, was a comfortable silence. The sun was heading downward and a cool breeze swept over Jim's legs. The wind on Mission Bay would be perfect.

THE LAST TIME

Early on, Husband #1 told me each of his hands had a specialty.

"This," he held up his right hand, "is my skill hand. The other is strength."

During sex I positioned myself on what I thought was the skill side, hoping for something better. But I must have heard him wrong because nothing changed. For months, I switched back and forth until finally I gave up.

By the time that marriage ended, my first of three, sex was reserved for special occasions or blackmail. One of the many low points of my life was when Husband #1 offered to buy me a pair of boots in exchange for a blow job. I acquiesced and tried to make a joke of it, flushing with embarrassment over the state of our marriage.

The last time I saw him, driving away with a bungee cord holding his car trunk closed, he smiled and said, "I guess we were too young." I nodded, knowing it didn't matter how old we were; it would have always ended this way.

Determined to start fresh, I moved to a city where no one knew me or Husband #1. I tried yoga, colonics, wheatgrass, and Christianity. Next was acting class. That's where I met Husband #2, who was five years younger, nearly a virgin, and called me his muse.

The first time I saw him on stage, he played a filthy hermit shot by the townspeople at the end of the second act. A gun went off and he disappeared through a trap door. I cried out across the dark theater. The person behind me laughed but it hardly registered. We'd only been dating six months but seeing future Husband #2 drop out of sight filled me with loneliness.

Two days later, after a bottle of wine and candlelight dinner, I bent on one knee and asked him to marry me. He was so flustered he said yes and, before he knew it, we'd been to the jewelry store and City Hall and home again, all legal.

A year later I sat in my shrink's office, asking if she thought it was me.

"Of course it's you," the doctor said. "Isn't that why you're here?"

"But we love each other," I said. "Shouldn't that be enough?"

"Was it enough for your first marriage?"

"We didn't have anything in common. This one—we have lots of things in common."

"Like what?" she asked.

I opened my mouth to answer but the question rattled around in my brain. We had both abandoned acting and nothing had replaced it. The day after the wedding, Husband #2 stopped playing the starving artist and applied to law school.

"I need a proper career to support a wife and family," he told me.

I smiled until realizing he was serious.

"You know I am an only child," he said. "I'm thinking four or five."

I saw the look in his eye that day as he surveyed the house, the car, me. I was no longer his muse and I thought a psychiatrist could tell me how to feel about that.

"I should want all that, right?" I asked her. "Don't I keep getting married in order to find a husband and settle down?"

"I don't know. Is that the reason?"

"I know it should be."

"But is it?"

I left her office without answering. That night I booked a trip to France, telling Husband #2 that I needed one last hurrah before launching our new life together. He helped me pack, tucking a pregnancy magazine into my suitcase.

In a hotel room in Paris, a man named Etienne sucked my toes as I called Husband #2 and told him to return to acting.

Husband #3 came along after a few years of one-night stands and three-month flings. This seemed, to all accounts, typical for a twice-divorced, manageably attractive, thirty-two-year-old woman.

The dating was easy—all my friends knew someone between thirty and forty years old. My only litmus was that he had to have at least one marriage behind him. After Husband #2, I didn't want to have to explain what marriage really was.

The one-night stands took very little effort. It's not difficult to be well-groomed, eloquent and interesting for one evening and sometimes the next morning. Three months, though, became tricky. At each three-month mark—after the realities of morning breath, running errands and meeting his family—I had to make a decision. Was he just a fling or Husband #3? Because, I told myself with the utmost sincerity, the third one would be the last.

I didn't have the heart to break up with future Husband #3 after three months. He really was too good to let go. He was, in fact, the best person I had ever met.

After sixteen months, I exhaled with relief as we tied the knot on a cruise ship among two hundred strangers. The slate was wiped clean and I was reborn, a newborn dipped into the sea of faith.

Husband #3 donated to charity. He volunteered as a Big Brother. When I cried, he wiped my tears, and when I felt randy, he rocked me like an all-star. Like clockwork.

There was no talk of children and we agreed on everything. It took me nearly a year to realize how annoying this was. I reassured myself that this was what marriage really was — effort and security. A partnership. Ying and yang. It was okay to be boring, I told myself. That's how things were accomplished.

After twenty-eight months, I finally admitted the truth to myself: I was a sprinter, not a marathoner.

I approached Husband #3 as he sat on the couch in the low afternoon light. I stood still, taking him in, until he noticed me.

"What are you up to, sweet cheeks?" He muted the television.

"We'll be doing this the rest of our lives, won't we?" I asked.

I sat next to him. He took my hand in his meaty one. Since the wedding, he gained fifteen pounds and stopped saying "bless you" after I sneezed. None of this mattered but I needed something.

"I know what this is about," he said.

"You do?"

"I saw the way you looked at me. Just now. The way you always look when I watch TV. You think I don't see you."

"I don't mean to judge…" I tried to regain my focus.

He patted my hand. "It's okay."

"No," I said. "You're too good for me."

"You make me good," he replied.

I pushed him away, unable to bear his lies about my own virtue.

On my fortieth birthday, I remained at a bar in the neighborhood long after the various friends and ex-flings I attracted like lint had gone home.

Just before last call, an old friend came in. He was an on-and-off lover and a good friend. In town for the weekend, he was always in the mood for a social call. I sat at a corner table by the defunct jukebox.

"Where did everyone go?" he asked.

"Husbands and babies and careers."

"And you?"

I shrugged. "I'm the life of the party."

"I know that." He reached across and fingered my bracelet. "That's pretty. New?"

I shook my head.

"You know what I did today?" he said. "Made my will. Lock, stock and barrel."

"That's a nice birthday wish," I laughed.

"It made me think of the last time with you." He signaled to the bartender. "Out of my whole damn exciting life, you are my one big regret."

I laughed again.

"No really," he said. "I think, if we weren't so juvenile, we could have been real. Not," he waved his hands around, "just doing this every six months."

We sat in silence for a moment, thinking about what held us, or didn't hold us, together. I twirled the bracelet around my wrist, trying to remember who had given it to me. All I could recall was that it had come in a blue box.

When the bartender called, my friend rose to retrieve our drinks. I watched him move across the room, noticing the perfect break of his pant legs over his expensive shoes. The full head of hair; the firm belly under his neatly pressed shirt. I felt the guilty pleasure of knowing he had at least one regret in his life.

"What do you think?" He handed me a drink.

I wondered if he expected me to run away with him. "Nice to know you think about me when I'm not around," I said.

"Why not make a go? The last time. That was something, wasn't it?"

I smiled. It *had* been something—bracing but comfortable. Like rediscovering lemon sorbet after years of chocolate ice cream. But it was too late for Husband #4. No one would believe me anyway.

"You're very sweet." I placed my hand on his arm. "But I think, either way, my destination would have been the same. You would have just been a different route."

He raised his glass and smiled. "Happy birthday, anyway," he said after a moment.

We sat there long past closing. As the bartender turned off the lights, I felt the beginnings of peace. Not because my life would be different, but that at some point it could have been.

ACKNOWLEDGMENTS

My deepest thanks to Kevin Morgan Watson and Press 53 for giving my book a home and literally making my dream come true. Thank you also to the editors of the literary magazines who published these stories individually. Thank you to the universe for leading me to Goddard College, which was exactly what I needed when I needed it. Thank you to all my Goddard advisors, especially the inimitable Rebecca Brown, program director Paul Selig, and friends and peers, gifted writers all, especially Chris Mackowski, Tim Kenyon, Val Carnevale, Kal Rosenberg, Kevin Rabas, and everyone from Clockhouse Writers Conference. Thank you to my San Francisco crew for their friendship and support, Laurel Flynn, Melissa Castro, and Walter Armer, with special gratitude to Sandra Cook, Noel Barnhurst, and Mark Gaspar. Much love to my best friend Donald Stahl-Ricco, who has been there longer than anyone, and his family. Thanks to my parents, Ned and Joan McConnell, and my in-laws, Shirlee and Ted Doron. And especially to Dan, who has read every word, been my biggest champion, and never doubted for a moment.

A native Californian, JEN McCONNELL began her writing life in San Francisco in 1996. She received her MFA in Creative Writing from Goddard College in Vermont. She has published numerous stories in literary journals and anthologies. Jen currently makes her home on the Lake Erie shore, with her husband, child, and pugs. She supports her writing habit by working in non-profit marketing and communications. Her website is www.jenmcconnell.com.

CPSIA information can be obtained
at www.ICGtesting.com
Printed in the USA
BVHW031533220720
584327BV00003B/220